I0758039

# THE RAIN WILL WASH AWAY THE BLOOD

BY WALTER HORSTING

Library of Congress 9-454-473 December 2, 2024



ISBN: 979-8-9885434-4-8 (Hardcover)

ISBN: 979-8-9885434-5-9 (Paperback)

ISBN:  979-8-9885434-0-4 (EPUB)

# Dedication

I dedicate this book to my gorgeous ex-fiancée, Sherry.

# Acknowledgments

*Mild Mannered Men* is a book of fiction painted on a historical canvas of high-technology companies and Northern California locations.

I started writing *Three Mild Mannered Men* on the way to Rome for my year abroad at age 14. At the home of fashion icon Rosana Pistolese, I told the dinner party about my spy yarn. Her brother Francisco declared over dinner that I must write a comic strip for his paper. The paper hired an illustrator whom I rejected for publication the following year. This book is a bridge to my past.

I want to thank my half-brother JR for his countless hours helping me. My half-sisters Amy, Jessie, and her husband, Russ, Ken Nicholson, Bob Tetz, and Rob Urbino, for their editing guidance. A shout-out to my music mentor, Dehner Patten, for toiling through my first draft. And my sister Archana started me on an art collection path.

Lastly, thanks to my loving wife, Sherry, for putting up with the many hours it has taken to finish the novel.

# Contents

# About the Author

At age nineteen, Walter Horsting started his first career as a teenage soundman in the music industry and formed a concert audio company. He engineered over three thousand live shows in ten years.

Walter branched into media systems integration of government hearing rooms, military command rooms, entertainment complexes, and Fortune 500 headquarters.

He has developed national and international business for leading media and technology providers for airports, smart cities control rooms, network control centers, and global briefing centers.

Walter lives with his wife, Sherry, in Sacramento, California.

**Principal Characters**

John Nord – Video Conferencing Manager

Laura Goodthing – John Nord's Girl Friend - RN

Jim Kelly – Conference Technician

Peter Holland – Upside Reporter

Jean Lovely – Peter's Ex-Girlfriend

Harry Harper – Upside Editor

George Camper – Encryption Investor

Happy Camper – Mergers and Investments

Mike Murphy – FBI Special Agent

Tim Thompson – FBI Special Agent in Charge

Frank Holden – FBI Special Agent

Joe Brick – SFPD Homicide

Sergei Marcov – Ex-KGB Agent

Boris Morozov – Marcov's Second

Dimitri Petrov – Sergei's Driver

Vulakovich Lopatin – KGB Station Head

Andrei Laskin – KGB Freelancer

Igor Levin – KGB Freelancer

Jorge Esparante – Sinaloa Cartel

Enrico Catalina- Jorge's Assistant

Miguel Cruz – Sinaloa Captain

Qiang Chen – China's Minister of Industry

Rupert Lee – Intel Chip Designer

# Prelude

*"Dignity of human nature requires that we must face the storms of life."*

**– Mahatma Gandhi**

*"No one would have crossed the ocean if he could have gotten off the ship in the storm."*

**– Charles Kettering**

The pineapple express assaults the California coast. An atmospheric river three thousand miles long lays siege to the Golden State. The clouds stretch beyond Hawaii. The jet stream steers the mass of moisture over the Pacific. A cold air front from Alaska builds a wall within the Great Central Valley anchored by low pressure, hovering over Monterey Bay.

The prevailing torrent of air forced northward and out of its undulating sidewinder like pattern becomes an artist's knife following a straightedge, cutting across the state, leaving the San Francisco Bay Area in the sunshine. The storm stalled over the Santa Cruz Mountains, a coastal mountain range of Central California. With nowhere to go, the band of heavy moisture-laden clouds released their burden.

# Santa Cruz Mountains

## 1999

### Above Felton in the Santa Cruz Mountains

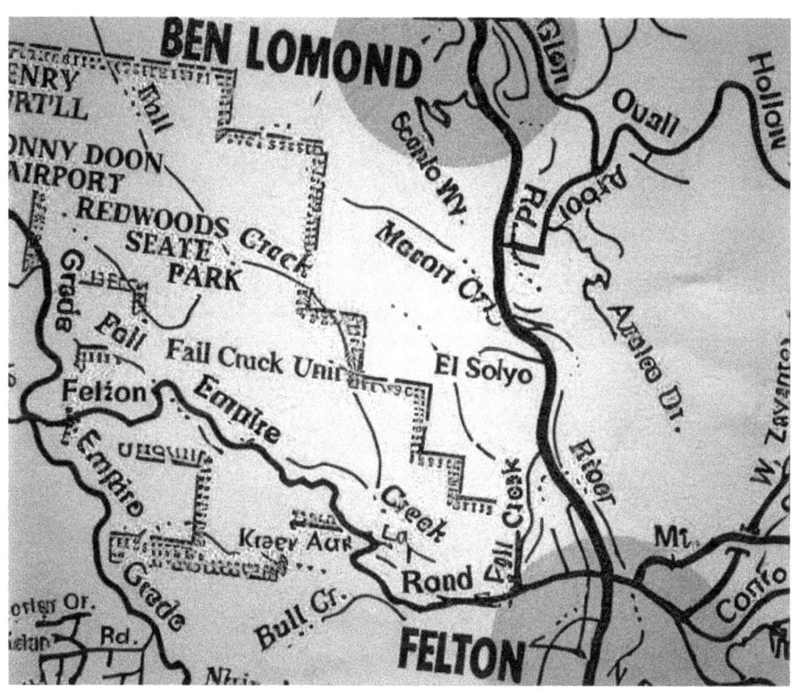


The monsoon gale was relentless, tearing apart the redwood trees that dotted the sweeping curves of Henry Cowell Redwoods State Park. Traffic was minimal, with only a few drivers braving the hundred-year storm that assailed the Santa Cruz Mountains that day.

## Mount Herman Road

The storm was brutal. John Nord squinted through the moving windshield wipers; his brows drawn with tension. The visibility was close to zero. He was clenching his jaw, angry at how the wipers were not quick enough, even at their fastest.

The rain came down in sheets, thundering on the roof of John's faded blue Taurus Wagon. His car swerved on the deserted but slick curves of the road, the winding asphalt reflecting the wagon's headlights at him. The midday sky was heavy with dark clouds, the torrential rain blinding every driver on the road.

The world beyond the shelter of John's car was pure chaos. The noise of the storm hemorrhaging through the car's windows. Even though the windows muffled the sound, John was fully aware of the creaking as the redwoods bent under the pressure of the wind.

## Felton Empire Grade Curve

The roadbed spiraled around consecutive two hundred and seventy degree turns while clawing another one hundred feet of altitude; sheets of rain pelted the road and hillside.

The wind whipped redwoods side to side, and the raging gale edged up in pitch and fury. Massive trees groaned in protest. Branches snapped in the wind, the redwood needles adding to the hell that poured down the Felton Empire Road curve.

The sound of heavy wind in an evergreen forest had its own fierceness. The high-pitched growl of trillions of needles scratching the air mixed with the guttural low-frequency strain of heavy timber, stretching to survive, foretold doom. A large branch slashed across the road and down the cliff along the side of Felton-Empire Grade.

The roadway rose two thousand tortuous feet from the foot of the grade. Hurricane-force winds lashed and moaned from the forest above the pavement as it twistingly ascended through a nasty corner. No one should be out driving, but John had no choice.

**Mount Herman Road**

"This is Santa Cruz classic rock. It is a wonderful day to stay indoors with another classic from Yes, *Owner of a Lonely Heart.*

The DJ's voice crackled through the radio. The song's instrumental began to bleed through the speakers of John's car. The riff of the electric guitars was easy to hear, even over the noise of the heavy rain. The blue wagon sped away from the Highway 17 exit. Mount

Herman Road wedged itself between the competing strip malls of Scotts Valley. John ignored the discordant symphony of horns behind him, protesting his driving.

John focused on another vehicle that zoomed in and out of the midday traffic ahead of him. The black sedan he followed sped past cars on the four-lane highway, snaking through the rush of traffic as John stepped on the accelerator in anxious pursuit.

The DJ's voice broke into the song's flow.

"Folks, we have a breaking story. A national weather alert for the Santa Cruz Mountains, torrential rain for the next six hours, and a landslide warning. Back to Yes."

*"Move yourself,"* the singer belted.

John's eyes darted to the signboard above, making a mental note of how soon Mount Herman Road would leave Scotts Valley behind. The sedan sped forward smoothly, unaffected by the torrential rain. John's faded blue wagon whizzed past five more cars, jumping ahead of traffic before the stoplight turned green.

The road began to narrow as the chase continued, the four lanes shrinking to one going uphill. John scanned ahead for the sedan, squinting through the downpour.

He spotted the dark sedan pulling past a fuel tanker truck beginning its slow ascent uphill. John gritted his teeth in frustration, staring at the sedan fast disappearing in the rain.

*"Never thinking of the future. Prove yourself,"* the song continued.

In his rush to catch up with the sedan, John almost missed the tanker changing lanes. He winced at the wrenching sound of metal against metal. The scrape was a sickening contrast to the rock song. Still, his car sped forward. John straightened up in his seat checking the damage his wagon had sustained.

The hauler had clipped the Taurus, taking the right turn signal with it. John veered right, narrowly escaping a collision with an oncoming logging truck. As he returned to his lane, the logger angrily sounded his air horn. The headlights behind him were blinding, the truck's beam set high.

*"You are the move you make.*
*Take your chances, win, or lose.*

*See yourself. You are the steps you take.*
*You and you, and that's the only way."*

The downpour got heavier as the road narrowed. The wind and rain had increased to hurricane strength. Branches snapped, and mud oozed over the road. Sludge began covering the inside lane as the howling wind increased.

Inside the Taurus, John, a rough handsome man in his thirties, ran a hand through his blonde hair, puffing out his cheeks as he exhaled. His gaze darted frantically to the mirrors, checking his position on the hill. His heart still thundered from the near-death experience of almost totaling his wagon into a logging truck. He was feeling the strain of the high-speed chase.

John sped after the dark sedan. It was the only thing he could do. His hand fell for his phone as he kept his gaze on the road, glancing down in time to see that it would not turn on no matter how many times he pressed the button on the side.

*"Shake…"*

The car veered sideways again as John's eyes darted around for the car phone charger. The charger he kept on the dashboard slid off onto the passenger side floor, out of reach.

John grunted, annoyed. The charger thumped against the soft makeup case his fiancée had kept there. He glanced down to see a nail file and cuticle clippers peeking out from the case. The passenger side was a mess of clutter, as if the woman who sat there would return any moment, gather her things, and pass John a smile and a wave as she headed off to work.

A Sutter Healthcare security pass slid out from her purse on the floor beside the case. John's throat tightened at the sight of the face staring back at him from the badge.

The sound of the truck horn faded into the downpour. John swallowed sharply, dropping the phone in his lap while pressing down on the gas, willing his car to speed up.

*"Shake yourself..."*

The rain hammered down on his windshield. John turned up the wipers' speed, clearing the windshield for a millisecond before the view returned to a blur of rain and the heavy wind. The redwoods bent whichever way the wind pleased, and the thunderous crackle of smaller trees falling and branches snapping leaked into the safe shell of John's car.

The redwood trees moaned as the rain blew sideways, cracking as nature continued its violent assault. Muddy rivulets trailed down into the roadway.

*You're every move you make.*
*So, the story goes, owner of a lonely heart."*

The narrow path had turned into a steep incline. As John urged his car up the slope, the faded Taurus battled against the wind and rain. He tightened his grip on the steering wheel, knuckles white as his jaw ached, his fiancée's face flashing before his eyes.

He had to make it.

*Owner of a broken heart.*

*Owner of a lonely heart."*

John let out a heavy breath as his faithful Taurus pulled through. The windshield cleared again momentarily, and John's eyes widened at the sharp curve ahead. The slick roadways would make it impossible to make it through in one piece. John clenched his jaw, determined as he turned the wheel, whispering a silent prayer as he felt the rear wheels slide on the turn slewing off the road entirely for a moment.

John held his breath, his heart stammering as the wheels floundered, barely staying on the road as he entered the town of Felton.

*"You've been hurt so before; watch it now.*

*The eagle in the sky.*

*How he dancin' one and only, you, lose yourself.*

*No, not for pity's sake; there's no real reason to be lonely.*

*Be yourself."*

The blue wagon slid to a rolling stop at Gramhill Road as he caught his breath. The chase had started taking a toll on him, but it was up to him. John's head whipped toward the right, gaze zeroing in on his target. The dark sedan was speeding away, unaffected by the storm. John stepped on the gas, shaking his head, his car rocketing away in pursuit.

*"Give your free will a chance.*

*You've got to want to succeed—owner of a lonely heart."*

The blue wagon crossed Highway 9 onto Felton Empire Grade at a breakneck speed. The car veered left and right; John was understeering to get his vehicle under control. John caught his breath as his car straightened. He felt the tension in his shoulders, the steady ache that increased with every passing moment. A battered green pickup truck on Highway 9 spun out of control at the light. Most drivers were pulling their cars onto the side of the road at awkward angles, not wanting to drive in blinding dangerous conditions.

John slammed his fist on the steering wheel, willing the car's exhausted, faded, battered remnants to push its limits for one more charge. He fought to steer left, the road both turning and rising as it curved uphill and steepened. John felt like he may as well have been chasing that sedan on foot. Steering the distressed Taurus was no less than a marathon.

The faithful wagon journeyed onward, the song's chorus continuing as the trees on either side had started to canopy the road John was on, supplying a temporary respite from the assaulting rain. John exhaled; his relief was short-lived as he took in the approaching hairpin curve.

*"After my own indecision, they confused me so.*

*Owner of a lonely heart.*

*My love said never question your will at all.*

*In the end, you've got to go."*

The rock song continued as John sped forward. No turn could scare him enough to stop his pursuit. Just then, a giant redwood branch fell onto the road. Spotting it in time, John avoided it, but the road ahead now seemed impassable. The wind whipped branches off strong redwood trees and laid them out crossways on the road. But John refused to slow down. He pushed the Taurus to its last limits, sweat beading on his forehead.

John muttered a silent curse as a branch landed heavily on the roof of his car.

Up ahead was a sharp turn that veered left, then right, with fifteen miles an hour posted.

*"Look before you leap—owner of a lonely heart.*

*And don't you hesitate at all - no, no."*

As the song faded into a guitar solo, John stared at his next challenge: the hairpin corner.

The roadway snaked through a series of turns. The rain softened the shoulder of the mountain opened to a ravine below. He steered a centerline through the extreme right hairpin as the pavement descended into the Redwoods. The water poured down the hillside in torrents that became gushing creeks.

John Nord nodded to himself, determined. He slammed his foot down on the pedal as the dark sedan sped seamlessly toward the turn, disappearing around the turn raising wakes of road water.

*"Owner of a lonely heart.*

*Owner of a lonely heart.*

*Much better than a*

*Owner of a broken heart.*

*Owner of a lonely heart."*

The road straightened slightly out into rhythmic curves. The wagon strained against the weather, the rasping sounds from the engine a sure sign of the price the chase cost the wagon. The straining engine mirrored John's mental state, the faded Taurus manifesting the intensity of its driver's panic, fear, and determination.

John floored it. The chorus of the song repeated, inching toward the end.

*"Sooner or later, each conclusion,*

*Will decide the lonely heart.*

*Owner of a lonely heart.*

*It will excite; it will delight."*

The song faded into silence as John approached another yellow fifteen-mile-per-hour sign leaning to the left. The storm bent the pole planted into the ground. The road spiraling up to the left, the slick road ahead had large cracks across the surface, promising him a harrowing experience.

*"It will give a better start.*

*Owner of a lonely heart."*

The music faded, John's panic winning out as he braked hard for the hairpin turn. The wagon dropped into the large crack in the road, jerking his body as the sun visor popped down. John felt the jolt run through him, his head slamming back against the headrest.

*Don't deceive your free will at all.*
*Don't deceive your free will—owner of a lonely heart.*
*Don't deceive your free will at all,*
*Just receive it—*

John sighed, gritting his teeth, reaching over, switching off the radio.

The blue wagon drifted through the hairpin curve and raced around the sweeping blind turn as the rain saturated hillside mud slipped down into the valley. The dark sedan disappeared while John, caught in the unforgiving road collapse, slid into the abyss.

In defeat, John pounded the steering wheel.

"And I thought I had it made."

# The Meeting

### Four Days Earlier, San Francisco

It was early morning, and the blue Taurus wagon was speeding down empty Bush Street past the Stockton Garage. A silver Infinity kept pace with the wagon and the timed lights into the Financial District. The pavement was still wet from last night's downpour; trash bins crowded the roadway for collection.

Max Roland, Maxy to his Castro Valley gay friends, set out on his morning jog to his work at the trading desk in the Bank of America Building. In his early thirties, he was jogging in a red and white tracksuit on Montgomery Street for his morning ginseng Tea and Dumplings in Chinatown. He absentmindedly crossed Bush Street, listening to Wham through his headphones.

The blue wagon braked hard and spun 360 degrees on the wet slippery intersection.

Maxy continued jogging.

The blue wagon slid through the intersection of Montgomery until it stalled. He almost collided with a Q45 silver sedan in a wild spin that came to rest next to the wagon.

John exchanged looks with the driver in Infinity, both shaking their heads in dismay.

Ten blocks later, the Taurus' tailpipe emitted pale blue smoke as it pulled into the Embarcadero parking garage with an early bird parking sign. The wagon nearly collided with a compact car exiting the garage.

John Nord finished parking the car in the Embarcadero lot. As he locked the doors, he realized he had left the keys to the vehicle. In his early forties, the man driving the Infinity parked nearby seemed annoyed and angry at him as John walked toward the elevator with an apparent limp. His laptop case and leather bomber jacket both showed signs of wear. The man's voice echoed in the empty garage.

**Peter Holland**

Peter is a six-foot-two-inch-tall man who resembles a young Harrison Ford. Peter started his day by ending his relationship with Jean Lovely, a wealthy art collector, and young widow. She was needy, demanding, and controlling. They met years ago in New York when he studied journalism at Columbia and worked part-time in a Chelsea art gallery catering to the wealthy upper Westside New Yorkers.

Jean was recently divorced from a Wall Street investment banker and had a condominium on the upper west side of the park. She was well off and used to the finer things her wealth entitled her to. Peter was attracted to her great look, willowy body, and fathomless depths of wanton sexual pleasures.

She wanted more than a life with a young writer and sought greener pastures with men. Peter could still hear her dismissal when she returned from a vacation in Belize, where she met her next husband. "Peter, it's over, and I won't have to put down the toilet seat anymore."

Peter graduated from Columbia and moved to the Bay Area to help his sister with high-end art sales in the East Bay. As a writer, he qualified for a below-market condominium in an artists' loft off 45th Street and Horton in Emeryville.

Several years ago, Jean reached out to him after he published an article that resulted in a takedown of the Thomas Kinkade empire, a follow-up to an exposé on Walter Keane, revealing the valuable "Keane Children" collection were painted by his wife, Margaret. Jean had lost her older, second husband to a heart attack.

She was ready to paint a new canvas and revisit their relationship. The expired husband had been an investor in chip plants, aerospace, and Apple.

Sex was not a problem for Peter and Jean on their first date after dinner. Jean dropped her dress in the foyer of her Pacific Heights home and took Peter. He then was expected to escort her to the Opera and openings at the de Young Gallery, where she served on its board of directors. Peter strained at the bit she ensnared him with access to the movers and shakers of the Bay Area. This is when he started his financial alert business. He was not above using his elevated level of access to his benefit.

But he was on her leash, and he resented it. He allowed her to buy him his Q45 when his Austin Healey blew an engine rod. When he left for work that morning, he deliberately left the toilet seat up.

Peter stood in the back of the parking garage, talking into a mobile phone pressed onto his left ear. He was alone, speaking in a flustered tone.

## MILD MANNERED MEN

"Jean, I said it is over; I've got to cover a story; I'll call you at lunch."

It was an unfinished argument that he had no desire to continue. He purged Jean from his thoughts by his need to cover a story on time. As a reporter, he enjoyed the thrill of a chase. As a journalist, he was a bloody mastermind who knew all the secrets of the town. Peter's job was to quickly reach newsmakers and break a story, and he excelled at finding good stories on his own. Through years of building relationships, he had the right contacts with many of the most impressive men and women in technology.

He knew what he was after; his ears perked up whenever a merger, financial crime, or bribe occurred. He always showed up before the others. He knew confidential details of the regulators, real estate deals, what happened in the halls of government, and who would appear next under the breaking news headline. He was responsible countless times for leaking information when the timing suited him.

Peter was always a shadow behind the scenes in his trench coat and an EOS-3 camera safely kept in the back of the vintage canvas backpack he carried everywhere. He always kept a notepad, filled with keywords. The real stories were developed in his mind.

He knew the tricks, techniques, and words that could spice up the details he collected. He ensured that his work was consistently ranked at the highest to remain at the top of his game. He cut the first bullet point he had written if it needed to sound more exciting.

"Shit," he muttered, clipping the phone to his belt as he left the parking garage.

## Hyatt Regency

*The Hyatt Regency Embarcadero Conference Center is a modern and popular meeting facility. It occupies the ground floor of the iconic downtown hotel. The center's clientele runs the gamut of the Bay Area's most influential high-tech and financial firms. Its location at the edge of the financial district makes it a popular site for video teleconference meetings.*

John entered the reception lobby of the Hyatt Convention Center. It was a space with indirect lighting and echoing acoustics. A buzz of conversation bounced off the marble walls with no definite source. A bank of clocks displayed time zones around the world, emphasizing the importance of synchronized time. A corridor led left from the lobby to a shared kitchen, where John prepared his daily shot of espresso.

His eyes met with Jo's as he entered the offices. She was a cute Asian receptionist who worked in administration. She had a soft smile and fluid brown hair shining under the fluorescent lights.

They spoke every time he entered the office.

Jo smiled politely and said, "Hey, John, I am glad you made it in early. Camper's press briefing shifted to the Grand Ballroom. They are expecting a large gathering of reporters who will need the big press feed."

John nodded in her direction, acknowledging what she said while holding out his laptop case.

"Can you keep this under your desk?"

"Sure. One more thing," she said as the laptop case disappeared. "A last-minute booking this morning for Sergei Marcov; he is in the Golden Gate Room. He needs a four-way call by eleven."

John discreetly rolled his eyes in annoyance. He did not want Jo to know how he disliked her directions, telling him what to do. He left the lobby to meet Mr. Marcov in the Golden Gate Room. Sergei Marcov was a tall, formidable-looking Slavic man,

Russian, John thought. He was well-dressed with gelled black hair, and in his early sixties with a long scar on his left cheek. He had rough hands and a receding hairline asserting his years of experience in battles of the past. He looked exactly like the powerful man he was. His heavy coat was a cashmere, his platinum ring was undoubtably expensive. Sergei's stared as John entered the room, a look John found threatening. John did not want to get on the wrong side before he could even say hello.

Sergei stepped forward to meet John as he arrived. His limp was noticeable.

As if on cue, Sergei pointed toward his leg and said, "Afghanistan."

*Sergei remembered the incident fourteen years ago when a stinger missile took down his Hind Gunship. He led his special forces team that fought with the Mujahideen. These fighters fired away with AK-47s, killing his comrades who endured the crash. Sergei survived by pulling the corpse of one of his men on top of him. He had a deep gash on his face as he lay amongst the dead men with a broken leg.*

John pointed toward his leg and said, "Panama."

John had his own memory of *the PDF guerillas retreating into the airport hangar. John had made contact on his radio when two rounds hit him.*

They look at each other with shared respect. John was more troubled by the request than the man.

"I understand you need a four-way call by eleven. That leaves me little time." John said.

"Lines must be encrypted and secure!" Sergei said smiling. He handed John a sheet of paper. "My locations, be a big tip for you," replied Sergei controlling the situation with his strong stance and raised brows; nobody dared to question him.

Sergei's list was on St. Francis Hotel stationery. Sergei walked out of the room. John hesitated a few moments before heading over into the Grand Ballroom. John noticed the tables, chairs, and shimmery lights hanging by the walls from last night's banquet. *'It must have been great,'* thought John.

He had to transform this banquet setting into a room for a press briefing. John tapped Pedro's shoulder, who was supervising the room clearing.

"We need to set up a camera stand midway in the room. I want a three-foot stage, eight feet deep and twenty-four feet wide, with two stairs off the rear. "We need two circuits for lights and one for audio," said John lightly.

"Okay, John," Pedro affirmed.

"Set two sets of two lights at forty-five degrees to light the stage."

"Got it!" Pedro acknowledged.

After what felt like a job done, John walked out and dialed his phone, leaving a message for his girlfriend, telling her that he had accidentally locked his set of keys inside the car and asking if she could bring him the spare ones when they met for lunch.

John walked to a nearby jewelry store to pick up Laura's engagement ring while the guys set up the banquet room. When John returned, he checked the Ballroom to see if things were going accordingly. Almost ready, John returned to the video conference suite. He checked the monitors and the speakers to see if they worked fine. He wanted to make sure this meeting went well.

John knew something was happening to the network. Usually, the six ISDN lines supplied a 384 K transmission link in seconds. The Ascend inverse multiplexer had two solid lines and two intermittent, and God only knew where the fifth and sixth lines were. Earlier, John's laptop PC's diagnostic software confirmed the network problem.

A train had derailed fifteen-hundred miles away, severing a fiber trunk line along a southern causeway bridge. Hundreds of AT&T, MCI, and Sprint network operations staff were working to re-establish service. While John was in the middle of preparing everything, Jo's voice came on the intercom.

"John, line two, it's Level Three."

John picked up the receiver then punched line two. A Level Three operator said. "One of our T-3 trunks was severed on the Mississippi by a river barge accident that derailed a train. As a result, we are rerouting all the west traffic. A workaround is underway; I will keep you updated soon."

The news annoyed him.

John answered a call on line two —it was Jo reminding him "It's Laura's birthday today, isn't it?"

"Thanks, Jo. Can you get AT&T online? Their network just crashed on me."

"John, you need to buy a new car," said Jo, talking about Laura's birthday.

"I'm unsure if Laura wants me to buy a new car or a ring."

"A ring?" Jo said, surprised. "Are you going to propose to her?"

"That's my secret," replied John.

John walked into the conference suite, noticing a gorgeous tall, trim brunette conversing with Sergei in the hallway outside the conference room.

"Sergei, for this deal to work, we need the export licenses for the nanometer etching equipment," she said. "Chen has that taken care of," Sergei replied. "After this concludes, I must take you to St. Petersburg. My cousin can arrange a tour of The State Hermitage and the Fabergé Museum.

"I have always wanted to see the eggs. You are making it enticing, Sergei."

"Yes, you need to drop your rules and come away with me," Sergei concluded.

"Maybe."

The video conference was with Beijing, Moscow, and Guadalajara endpoints. The live video picture broke up, crashing and returning only to slow down to seven frames a second. John was on edge. The video teleconference started in ten minutes, and the extra layer of encryption needed was not helping. The audio needed lip-synching with the Guadalajara conference center at this slow transmission rate.

Sergei walked into the room, closing his cell phone.

"Da, da, I need to add four more sites. All are to be encrypted," said Sergei.

"I will set it up, but it will cost you a lot," replied John. "I need to order up more lines. At this late date, I am not sure we can find a conference bridge."

"Money is not a problem. I want it now, at once," said Sergei with urgency. His authoritative voice took control of the room; his wishes were a command. "I need to share my laptop's presentation on the call. Make it happen, big tip for you."

"I'll be right back with a video interface." John said, turning on his heel, anxious to make Sergei happy.

John returned with a computer scan to the video converter. The Extron Super Emotia with Genlock allowed the laptop's video image to be frame-stabilized with the video transmission after the computer interface tapped into the graphics signal of the laptop.

"No promises, but I will see what I can do." Sensing a bonus, John gave a thumbs up and crossed his fingers for his client's benefit.

Sergei's brow darkened as he waited for John to succeed.

*"Who could say no to that"?* Sergei said to the brunette, lighting a cigarette and taking a puff. To get what he wanted, he always offered the highest amount, was ahead of every curve, and always bet against the odds. Nothing was impossible for him, and he would happily ruin anybody's life who stood in his way. It was criminal.

"Sergei, honey catches more flies than vinegar," she answered.

"I am sorry, my sweet. I am used to command." Sergei said, "I will tip him generously for his trouble, OK?"

Fortunately, John was owed a favor by the network bridge coordinator at the Sprint Meeting Channel. He had bailed out Betty just last week with an earlier last-second multipoint rental for her client. Betty entered the wrong date on a booking, ending up double booked and out of capacity. As one of her former and regular customers, John readily agreed to lend her the use of his bridge until the Network Meeting Center bought an added 12-port multipoint bridge. He knew owing a favor would come in handy; he did not know how soon.

John made a call after he opened his laptop and changed the settings. However, Sergei grew upset as his laptop's video did not deliver a solid image; it was not working. The three built-in monitors on the wall displayed a beautiful dark-haired woman, an ageless Chinese man, and a Latin man who was bald and in his sixties.

Sergei's anger exploded as he saw the display and bellowed, "The picture is all wrong."

"It must be your video card's compatibility; we see this all the time. Let us put your CD into my laptop; I will have it up in one minute," replied John.

"Do it quickly. Ladies and gentlemen, the technician will get my presentation up soon. Go on, Chen," said Sergei, addressing the Chinese man on one of the monitors.

John's solution was to use his laptop's high resolution video card. He quickly removed the presentation disc from his laptop player and inserted Sergei's disc. He showed the controls to Sergei, but he dismissed John's gesture with a hand wave.

"Leave us; we need privacy!" Sergei ordered.

"Chen has excellent news, as do I," said Jorge.

"I have secured the export controls exemptions on the equipment, and they insist it will be suitable for sub .018 Micron devices," replied Chen.

"How did you get the exemptions so fast?" the woman asked.

"The White House was very friendly. It pays to sleep in the Lincoln Bedroom before each election," said General Chen. "Sergei, I will see you tomorrow for the signing."

"The best news for the last. BCCI will be underwriting our venture. I must apologize. I must end the call; I have another meeting," finished the woman, who got up from her seat then pulled on her raincoat. She faced the screen as she shouldered a slim purse over her coat.

"Happy?" Sergei looked at the American woman.

"Sergei, we will need to meet tomorrow for some concluding elements in the deal." She said, before turning to leave the room.

"Our shipments are on time, Happy," said Sergei right before the remaining video screens went black.

John enjoyed watching the brunette's trim form stride down the hall before entering the room and handed Sergei his bill. He removed Sergei's disc from the laptop and was about to put his disc into the player when Jo called over the intercom, informing him that Laura was on line four and wanted to talk to him.

John set the disc down and picked up the handset, punching line four.

"Hi, gorgeous!"

"I will be there soon. Can you come out? It is raining cats and dogs," said Laura, on her way to pick him up from work.

"Happy to, sweetie. Meet me at the side door. Did you bring my spare keys?" asked John.

"I sure did."

"Thanks! Give me ten minutes. My video conference just ended, and I need time to pitch my business plan to Mr. Camper."

Laura understood and would allow him his ten minutes.

After John ended his call, Sergei approached, handing him an envelope. John noticed a red stone Army Victory ring on his right hand, a big baroque commemorative ring. Sergei thanked him for his quick service and showed his gratitude.

"Thank you for jumping all the hoops today. I have my disc," he said.

"Thank you for using the Hyatt Regency Conference Center," replied John.

John was curious and peeked into the envelope and saw the massive tip in Benjamins. John picked up his disc and placed it inside a presentation folder and a manila envelope he carried. He made his way toward the receptionist's desk.

"Jo, I will be in the ballroom, the press conference is winding up, and I am doing the last rounds." John said, before adding, "Laura is picking me up for lunch."

"O.K. Happy birthday and good luck," Jo said.

"See you after lunch," John said as he left.

As John entered the Ballroom, he saw the news crews disassembling tripods, cameras, and floodlights on the camera platform. He saw Pedro and gave him the sign to 'cut off' the sound and lights motion with his hands. He quickly scanned the room, noting the reporters crowding the stage surrounding a middle-aged man waving to him, George Camper.

John made his way toward the stage, telling the staff supervisor, "Pedro, we have the Chamber of Commerce breakfast in the morning. Your crew needs one-hundred tables, and two buffet lines set up by the end of your shift."

"No problem, John!" Pedro pointed to the stage. "Mr. Camper needs your help."

George Camper wore a dark pin-striped suit and a red tie. He was the center of attention for a gaggle of reporters surrounding him, like sharks feeding on a dead whale. John made his way over.

"I'm John, the coordinator for Hyatt Business. Can I help you?"

"John? Thank God you are here. I need your help." Camper said. He looked suffocated by the press hemming him in.

"Follow me out through the kitchen." John led him out. George grabbed his coat and briefcase, following John out.

On the hotel loading dock, John finally got what he had been waiting for; the chance to share his business plan. Knowing he was sharing his idea to a powerful businessman like George Camper, John could not contain his excitement. John did not waste the moment.

"Mr. Camper. I trained in military encryption and installed video systems globally for the Joint Military Command. I wanted to hear your talk today, but another meeting came up. Would you look over my business plan for a secure collaboration network?"

"I do owe you for getting me out of there." George nodded to John to go on as Camper pulled on his trench coat.

John pulled out an envelope with his video and business plan outline and handed it to Camper. John watched him add it to his briefcase before he left. George promised he would get back to him the next day. Now all John had to do was wait and see how George would respond. He had done his part.

**Peter Holland**

The other journalists kept Peter from interviewing George Camper, pissing him off. The scrum of reporters blocked his path while he yelled for attention, "Mr. Camper, One question!" as a staffer led Camper out of the back of the banquet hall.

# The Campers

As the storm assailed the city, the sky darkened, and the rain got serious. Peter Holland, the *Upside* reporter, stood on the loading dock outside the ballroom, George Camper was not to be seen. Peter was determined to capture the lost opportunity. He had been getting shit from his editor about every piece he turned in since starting at *Upside*. At this point Peter was willing to do whatever was required to get his story.

He was tall, six-foot-two, and very fit. His face had the chiseled looks to get him a spot on a magazine front cover. He used his looks to his advantage when possible. Peter was not a typical reporter, and he never came off as one because of his appearance and charm. He cleverly slipped into the pauses of everyday conversations, disarmed his subjects, smoothed the rough edges of a reporter's direct approach.

He broke a story three months earlier about the drug trade creeping into Silicon Valley. There were copious amounts of cocaine and meth being traded for industrial secrets and expensive chipsets. That issue of *Upside* flew off the magazine racks and into the hands of the FBI and DEA. Peter, of course, could not divulge his sources even with the threat of jail. Harry, his editor, was pushing for a follow-up story, which he refused to do. Now, Peter was onto a giant headline.

Peter fell into a big story by accident a week earlier. During his morning scans of his personal Newspage, he noticed a story. Personal Newspage was an excellent free source of local news from Individual.com, allowing anyone to sort articles of interest and follow companies, development, real estate, or IT integration stories. Information Technology is what drove Peter Holland. The article outlined a coming shake-up of how people work and transact on the net.

Or on the other hand, IT was the sandbox of darker forces on the net: hackers, thieves, and enemy states. The press release was SOP, Standard Operating Procedure, for startups. Announce an innovation, grab the higher ground of mind share of the software business, tactics used by Microsoft and others for years. He had leapt at the bait for this trolling tactic once before with the MS Money versus Intuit battle. Peter knew how to call around to see what he could find out about the forces driving MS into a premature announcement. A friend of his, a VP in business development at Cisco, steered him onto the trail that led him here, to Camper's press conference.

Inside the Hyatt conference center, Peter took the escalator up into the second-floor 12-story atrium. He walked toward the restaurants beyond the massive art installation that echoed a Woolite Logo. He held his phone with his left hand, gesturing with his right hand as he talked to his editor, Harry, was exasperated and equally disappointed about the missed chance.

"I was about to shake hands with him, Harry, and some staffer led him out through the kitchen. I just lost him," Peter said, knowing what came next.

"The story of the year. I should fire your ass!" Harry riled up and threatened him.

"And I will burn your house down! Then where would we be, Harry?" Peter lowered his voice, "I'll catch up with him, Harry." Peter reassured. Finally, the conversation reached a compromising end.

"OK, forget it. I will have my secretary set up an appointment for the interview. We will just pray he has time before the next Market collapse, Pete? When will I see the follow-up story to *Chips, Cocaine, and Coercion?*" Harry asked.

"Listen; the story we printed ended my access," Peter let that sink in before continuing. " But I am on to an even bigger story," Peter countered. "Internet security is a Trillion-dollar crime waiting to happen."

Harry hung up. Peter's phone went dead, and a grim expression appeared on his face. The words he had just heard stung, but he slung his trench coat over his shoulders. Peter's boots sounded against the tiles. Peter had a forceful walk, which became a habit as part of his everyday job, which was all about reaching locations quicker than the rest. Peter noticed the atrium's grand space; the vastness somehow diminished his troubles.

Looking at his watch and watching the last tables seated in the restaurant, Peter decided he had better find someplace to eat. With this rain, every table in the Financial District would be gone in minutes. Peter decided to eat down the street at a grill, he knew he would have decent food and Sierra Nevada Pale Ale.

He turned and descended the escalator to street level. Peter expected everyone and everything around him to work faster as well. The men were all dressed professionally, but no one carried an umbrella.

*'Didn't they know a rainstorm was forecast?' Peter thought to himself. 'Thank God I brought one.'*

The weather was lousy, the sidewalks jammed, and Peter was poked more than once by the oversized umbrella-wielding workers rushing to get lunch. *'It's going to be a mess,'* he thought. Peter hurriedly walked through the rain; his thin smile was interrupted by sharp prods beneath his black umbrella.

Pete had come a long way from his technology newsletter days. He broke the early AOL-Yahoo merger before AOL's offer to buy Time Warner. And before that, he helped track the transformation of Steve Jobs from Apple to NEXT to Pixar.

Battling underfunding and understaffing for fifteen years, publishing the most current weekly newsletter on Silicon Valley, his bulletins reached the top decision-makers worldwide. He hosted private affairs at top restaurants while wondering if there would be funds to pay the bills. It was always a stretch, and then it all came crashing down on him like a sack of wet cement. It was an ongoing struggle to make ends meet, and professional pride making up for lack of pay.

He had great insights into technology but needed to gain business management skills to take the business to the next level. He could still remember two solid months of fighting off the creditors and tax authorities while looking to the future. The pounding headache that denied him sleep for weeks. And then he landed this fantastic story on Microsoft, put it on Harry's desk at *Upside*, and finally, his work went on without all the headaches.

Then, there was Jean. Peter had to do something to streamline his life. He took out his phone, calling to leave a voicemail.

"Hi, Jean, I've thought it over; I can't take it anymore," he spoke gently, with his eyes closed and a heavy sigh. He was still deciding whether to add more or leave it at that. But before he could change his mind, he quickly added, "I feel like a Yo-yo with you. Yes, I know your efforts to make it work, but I am tired of trying." His phone's battery died, and he put it back on his belt.

He felt like he owed at least this clarification to Jean. Still unsure how she would react to it, Peter lengthened his stride toward a pub and slipped inside.

The Royal Exchange was a British-style pub on Front and Sacramento, kitty-corner from the Embarcadero Cinema. Peter was tired of Chevys and the trendy eateries in the four-block, mixed-use development. He liked the Pub's large windows overlooking Sacramento Street on the ground floor with faux pillars in Hunter Green with gold accents. Above its main windows, small windowpanes completed the detail. The Exchange's sign overhanging the entryway welcomed the customer with the sun logo. Full tables greeted the waterlogged reporter. Peter had to squeeze inside the door. The line for tables was out the door and into the rain. He took a glance inside the room. It was overcrowded, with the lunch crowd surging into the bar area.

Peter was hungry. With the tables full, it would be at least a thirty-minute wait. No one in their right mind was hurrying to slog through the elements again. He was drenched, a small pond forming around his ankles. He decided not to wait for a table, moving to the bar to order lunch.

Angling through the crowd, Peter approached one of the three remaining stools. Pete could not ask if the seats were open as the man beside him had his back turned, on his cell phone, holding a finger in his ear to block out the general din. It was clear why the seats were empty as they were next to the service area. He quickly took a seat before someone else.

He got a menu and asked for coffee instead of ale. Peter found an outlet for his charger, grabbed a Chronicle folded in half at the end of the counter, and settled in.

Peter looked up as he turned the page and noticed the tall, trim brunette lady enter the restaurant. Loaded for bear, she stood with an oversized black leather shoulder bag, umbrella, newspaper, Nordstrom shopping bag, and cell phone. She was a looker with a steely urban finish. Her cropped hair flowed back over her ears from a playful point high on her forehead. Her black trench coat, now open, revealed a fit body under her red silk blouse and black leather pants. She was looking for someone and appeared on edge, adjusting her baubles as if late for a date.

As soon as she spotted him, she moved to the counter to the man seated next to Peter.

"Hi, George!" she exclaimed as she moved closer, kissing him.

The man turned around, and to Peter's surprise, it was George Camper. Mr. Camper was as immaculate as the woman who took the seat next to him. He was dressed in a dark pin-striped suit, had sleek hair, and wore an exclusive-looking wristwatch, singling him out as an affluent man in the room.

"Hi, darling."

Peter was able to eavesdrop on their conversation easily.

"Sorry I am late; we had to add essential venture partners to the teleconference. Did you get my voicemail?" Happy asked, looking him straight in the eye.

"Yes, I did, but I had to give up our table. The press conference went well," George replied.

He quickly gave her more detail about the conference by adding, "The questions just kept coming…."

And soon, the flow of conversation shifted to what they should order for lunch. They exchanged more pleasantries and inquired about each other's days.

"There is a forty-minute wait for a table, and I am famished. Do you mind if we eat at the bar?" George asked.

Happy was hungry and nodded in favor as they lost themselves in the conversation. Peter was on the edge of his stool, listening to every bit of the exchange. Finally, she stood in the middle of the conversation and took off her trench coat, revealing a red silk blouse. accentuating her breasts. His gaze traveled between her breasts and hips as Peter appreciated Happy's abundant curves. The room got congested and heated as more people surged in.

Happy reached into her shopping bag and took out a box draped in fancy wrapping paper. She glided it across the counter for George to look at it.

"Here's Aunt Em's gift. I hope she likes it."

"Ah, thanks for getting it for me. I am taking Em to Twenty-Eight after my testimony at the Capitol tomorrow. Want to come with me?" George raised his eyebrows in question.

"I'd like to get away, but–" the sentence was interrupted when two elderly women dressed in St. John knit suits and blue-dyed hair entered the bar and sat next to George on recently vacated stools. They conversed loudly without breaks, making speaking harder for the Campers. They also hindered Peter's eavesdropping.

"Doris, I am paying for lunch this time," said the lady in blue.

"I'll pay for the movie and parking," replied the lady in green.

Peter leaned in some more.

Happy continued. "I will let you know in the morning. I am staying close to this deal; you know me with closing. It is complicated, commingled funds, transfer of equity, IP, global investors, and a technology transfer for a chip plant in China."

"Sure thing!"

"So, what's the big news?" Happy pushed the topic in another direction.

"At the press–" As George replies, the two elderly women laugh too loud. Peter missed that part of the sentence and then overheard Happy saying something.

"On second thought, I must drive the Chinese partner flying in to meet one of the players for the deal in Sacramento; I could tie it into cocktail hour. Let me work it out."

Peter stood up to remove his trench coat, and unfortunately, his Ericsson digital phone, still plugged into the charger, flew off his belt clip. The phone hit the floor, separating into the battery, keypad, and mouthpiece, with the parts tumbling under Happy and George's stools and making a racket. Happy and George turned around in surprise.

"Excuse me; this phone has the worst belt clip. Would you mind getting up? Some of my parts went under your stools?" Peter said as graciously as possible.

"You're missing your parts?" Happy teased as she winked at him, standing up. "Are you sure this isn't a pickup line?"

His confidence stood out to Happy, who flirtatiously asked him if this was a pickup line. He saw her gorgeous figure, nice waistline, all five foot nine inches of her, weighing 130 pounds, a tall glass of I-want-to-know-you.

"You found me out; I usually make a fool of myself attempting to meet a gorgeous woman. Honestly, I have had difficulty catching up to your husband." Peter uttered as he scrambled for his phone's pieces.

Peter confidently stood up and offered an apology. It was his chance to talk to George Camper; he would not miss it for the world. Peter took this as an opportunity to introduce himself.

"I am Peter Holland, and I work for Upside Magazine. I called your office yesterday, and Jill set up a meeting at the Hyatt after the press conference. I needed fifteen minutes of your time for a security article about Electronic Commerce I am developing," he uttered expectantly.

She eyed his daunting presence. "George, Mr. Holland can't be much of a reporter," she said in an overly friendly and teasing tone.

George took over the conversation. "Don't mind my younger sister," he shook his head at Happy, "She is used to getting more attention from young men than you're giving her!"

Peter's phone rang. He glanced at the screen, shook his head, and answered. "Hi, Jean. Yes, I will think it over."

"A man of mystery." Happy purred as the Maître d' approached.

"Mr. Camper, I had a cancellation. Are you still interested in a table?" asked the Maître d'.

"We'll take it," George answered, turning to Peter. "Peter, do you want those fifteen minutes?"

Peter followed the Campers.

**John and Laura**

Laura picked up John on California Street. She adjusted the rearview mirror, which reflected her blonde hair and pointy nose. Laura was a perky nurse who looked even sexier dressed in her uniform. She drove past Pine Street, passed a slow car, and settled behind a flatbed truck hauling steel I-beams. She suddenly swerved and braked the car to avoid hitting a car pulling into her lane. Her makeup case slid off the dash and into John's lap. The car stalled.

"Sorry about that. I caught my nail and made a quick fix while waiting for you. I was helping Mary turn an extremely heavy patient, and the bed frame bit me. It was easier when I worked at Shriners with small kids, but heartbreaking."

"Just keep getting help with the large patients; no need for both of us to be lame," John replied, attempting to protect her.

Laura restarted the car and pulled in closer behind the flatbed truck loaded with structural steel.

John cautioned, "Slow down! Do not get too close to that truck."

Laura jumped in her seat as she looked at him with her eyebrows raised in response. She needed clarification.

"What is wrong with you? Since when you became nervous with my driving?" she asked softly.

John's eyes glossed over, lost in a memory from five years ago. *He was driving a Honda on Interstate Five, ascending a long hill. John was racing through a sheer narrow cut on the hillside. He saw a looming I-beam in the middle of the road.*

Laura snapped her fingers in front of John, causing him to come out of his trance. "Where did you get lost?" she inquired.

"A couple of years ago, I was on Interstate Five in my Honda doing eighty-five in the fast lane, returning from an installation in Los Angeles. I was going up a long steep hill south of Patterson. I topped the pass; a forty-foot construction I-beam on its side was diagonally blocking the road from the fast to the slow lane."

"What did you do?"

"I knew I was dead if I hit it. I wanted to get it between the wheels. My car turned into a slot car racer, and I exited the beam in the slow lane going eighty-five. That is when I saw the two wrecks on the road."

Laura tutted, sympathetically.

"Since then, I've been driving much tamer and nervous."

## Tonga Room Restaurant

Lunch and the day were great; the one-thousand-dollar tip made John feel good about this week. The bonus paid off the balance on the ring he had in his pocket. They had been together for the past two years and living together for the past year. John felt strongly about building a life with Laura. They had common interests and upbringing; both were military brats who grew up worldwide.

You had to make friends fast when your parents transferred around the world. His dad was a Lt. Commander in the Navy, who taught night-flying-off-carriers during World War II and Judo to the troops. His mother was a nurse; there was always work for the commander's wife after the kids grew up.

Laura's dad was an Airforce Captain piloting C5s around the world. Travis AFB and the 349th were her dad's last assignments in the Reserves while flying for Southwest Airlines. That is how John met Laura. He went to the Annual Open House at the Base. After a horrific three-hour traffic jam, John finally got onto the Base. He reached the tarmac and was in front of the F-117.

# MILD MANNERED MEN

John looked forward to examining the F-117 Stealth Fighter and watching the Blue Angels show. In his earlier years at McClellan AFB, while with TASA, the Television Activities Support Authority of the US Military. The Sacramento Airbase was all hush-hush over the quiet plane flying over Elk Horn Road into the Sacramento base on moonless nights.

John supported the top-secret video system in TechOps 1040. Even though he had top-secret clearances, all screens and whiteboards were covered when he needed access to the room. Years later he learned what they did there.

The Base managed the logistics and maintenance for the Military's A-10s, F-111s, Tomcats, and the advanced chip design labs. The Base processed the fighters and routinely passed the fighters through the Neutron Imaging Beam to search for flaws internal to the wings and fuselage. John flew around the world from this Base, installing communication systems for the Joint Military Command. He had only seen the plane land from a distance. And this was his first time seeing the fighter up close and personal. If you would call the airmen with M-16s and shoot-to-kill orders enforcing a safe distance from the plane 'close.'

John turned around at the sound of the Blue Angels coming in low to the ground. As the pilots stood their jets on their tails and burst skyward into their famous starburst maneuver, John stepped back and tripped over Laura, kneeling, helping one of her nephews with an errant snow cone in his overalls. John tucked his shoulder in and rolled to the concrete. He was remarkably unhurt, except for his pride and dignity. Laura was wide-eyed at his wrestler's tuck-n-roll and was concerned about John's physical and mental condition. What a way to make a first impression, but they really hit it off.

Laura's mom had enough work at home, caring for four boys and Laura. Laura was a spunky girl and ran with the boys. They had built a resilient family that stayed in touch with each other. She looked like anything but a tomboy in her strapless cocktail dress last week at the Sutter Health fundraiser. The gown's emerald, green color was offset nicely by her blonde hair. She was cheerful and sharp, not a bad combination to wake up to for John. She also was not doing too badly in the income department. Laura was an RN at Sutter Health, and her investments in the company's 401K plan were likely to carry them through retirement.

At first, Laura tried to ignore it, but she could not help but worry about John. It was clear something was on his mind. He was looking but not seeing. They were seated at a lovely table at a fabulous restaurant, but John was elsewhere.

"John," she began softly. "You're distracted. What is on your mind? Work?"

His distant gaze refocused on Laura's face. He gave her a thin-lipped smile, "George Camper said he would look over my business plan. I could use a break."

She reached across the table to take his hand, "It will get better." Laura smiled, "You're one of the most intelligent men I know."

"It came off okay. I forgot something. But, hey, I was awesome, as usual, and I got a great tip after a rough start!" John tried explaining, "One of the lines went out."

John saw her eyes glaze, which was not the response he wanted. As an ICU nurse, she always cut to the chase of John's stories. He knew he was losing her patience and today was another one of those moments.

"I wanted to ask you a question," John said, reaching into his pocket.

"Before you do, John, I want to know where we are going?" Laura looked deeply concerned.

John swallowed, making every effort to get a read on Laura's expression. He reached into his pocket. His fingers were wrapped around a ring case just below the table.

**John and Laura's Rental**

Later that evening, the radio played softly in their bedroom, an acoustic guitar duet filling the air as John and Laura lay in bed. Laura curled up next to John, with a brilliant-cut, one-carat diamond ring glinting in the soft lamplight on her left hand. The radio played a gentle song.

*"Only now, you can sleep. Only now, you can dream away.*
*Tonight, you are safe in my arms.*
*Now I know deep inside.*
*There is no more to hide.*
*It's out of us both.*
*Now we can sleep.*
*Honey Sweet..."*

The duet faded, a gentle guitar solo floating above the lyrics as the song filled the air.

*"Now there is more than me.*
*So much now we can sleep in each other's hearts.*
*Now, we can sleep."*

Laura's eyes were wet, tears threatening to trail down her cheeks. "I always have worked and never thought I needed someone," she confessed, her voice thick with emotion. "I have never been happier, John."

John cradled her face, mirroring her watery, grateful smile. He planted a kiss on her forehead and then again, gently on her lips. Laura smiled into the kiss, her hands finding his torso, her body inching closer to his. The radio's music was a gentle addition as they made love.

# Day Two - El Indo, TX

In the blazing heat of the late afternoon sun, men at the Ranch El Indio in Texas loaded a drug shipment onto a heavy truck. The ranch was isolated, so the move took place in broad daylight. The truck's ten-ton load of cocaine was brought across the river on the backs of bicycles and wetbacks, hundred pounds per crossing, twenty trips per ton, and two hundred for this truckload.

His muchachos commandeered a farm thirty miles south of Eagle Pass, tied up the family, and spent the past two nights ferrying the drugs across the river. They offered the family a thousand dollars and told them to take it or die. They accepted the money with little argument. It was a good set-up, using thirty illegals to carry the drugs across the border. One weekend of work, a green card was waiting, and if someone got caught, it would not be Miguel.

**Jorge Esparante's Villa, Guadalajara, Mexico**

Jorge Esparante was a small, bald, thin Hispanic man in his sixties. As he walked across the enclosed garden of his villa on his way back from his tennis court and daily lesson, idly swinging the racquet in his right hand as he talked to someone on his cell phone. A red bandana kept the sweat from his eyes as he walked.

"Miguel, I need you to take care of some loose ends today."

**El Indo, TX**

The bodies of a rancher, his family, and his dog lay in the barn close to the truck loading. Miguel's right-hand guy, Ricardo, killed the family and retrieved the money they had been given. There had not been much of a struggle.

"No one will miss them for a while" Miguel said.

Ricardo walked over the bodies; indifferent as he poured gasoline over them. The gasoline trailed to the barn's entrance, where Ricardo dumped the can. He stood nearby, lighting a match. The setting sun matched the colors of the flames engulfing the barn.

Ricardo climbed onto the passenger side as Miguel drove the loaded truck from the farm.

**Highway 131**

After driving twelve miles, following the Rio Grande River channel northwest out of Eagle Pass on Highway 277, Miguel turns the truck onto Highway 131. The heavy truck bellows out a series of deep-throttled tones, downshifting. Four miles shy of Normandy, where 131 heads toward Spofford, twenty-four miles north. The large van was the only moving object in sight.

At 2 a.m., no other headlights were visible on the highway beside the truck's high beams, yet Miguel signaled and slowed, making a model turn north on Highway 131. The desert echoed with the guttural sounds of the truck's heavy diesel engine downshifting and pulling hard on the rise as the truck sped through Maverick County toward Spofford.

At this hour of the night, the abandoned roads and the desert offered little company or entertainment to the heavyset Mexican man that drove the truck.

Miguel was a thirty-five-year-old Mexican American, heavy set with a large belly that jiggled with each shift. He considered himself to be a professional driver. He wore well-used rawhide gloves on both hands. He shifted into second gear, leaving the split axle's large red button in low. He was pulling a full load this night. The driver could feel the power still in reserve as the International Harvester turbocharged engine pulled up the rise out of the river's ancient flood bed.

"It is a good time to drive in the desert," Miguel commented in his rasping and deep voice. "It is not so stinking hot; no cars and no cops."

Miguel's heavily tattooed arm was cooling in the wind. His expression was pure bliss. He maneuvered around a road-closed sign.

"Abusado! Ten cuidado!" howled Ricardo from the passenger seat.

The truck straightened after the corner. Miguel slammed the brakes when he spotted the Texas Highway Patrol Car blocking the highway. Muttering a curse, Miguel stopped the truck. They both eyed the police officer strolling toward the truck.

The officer shined his flashlight into the cab and then down the side of the truck. He also rounded the vehicle, flashing the torch underneath the truck's rear. Ricardo slowly reached for his Mac 10 with an attentive gaze as he watched the officer. Miguel seemed unfazed. He waved him down, signaling with his finger to keep the gun out of sight. He leaned out his window, "Que Pasa?"

The highway patrol officer met his gaze, finally breaking character, "Miguel, you are on time for once. Let's make it snappy."

Max Penwell was once an honest cop. However, after arresting Jorge Esparante two years ago, death threats and piles of money changed his mind. The evidence for Jorge's trial disappeared. Max did not have to kill anyone or smuggle any drugs. He only had to recruit a partner to block the other end of the road and allow the airplanes to land and leave undetected. His silence cost twenty thousand dollars per delivery. The income from two or more deliveries a month deposited in an offshore bank was about five times his trooper's salary having no taxes withheld.

"Pull it over there," Max pointed with the flashlight beam. The road closure was all performance for the public. The five-mile blockage of the highway kept any motorists from seeing or interfering with the landing of the airplanes. The planes Miguel was meeting were using the artery for a runway. The planes stayed especially low to avoid the Air Traffic Control Radar out of Laughlin AFB 35 miles to the north.

Miguel put the truck in gear, driving to the three planes parked on the road. He pulled across the highway, backing it in for unloading. As Miguel climbed down from the cab of the truck, one of the pilots and Enrico Catalina approached him.

"Miguel, do you have a light?" he asked. The pilot wore a cowboy hat on his head.

Miguel lit a match on the side of the truck and offered it to him. The pilot lit his cigarette, taking a long drag from it. The pilot nodded, inhaling.

"How much time to load?"

"We'll have you done in ten minutes," he answered. "Where are you headed?"

The pilot smirked as he walked away, "Where I can ski and gamble if the storm lets me land."

"You're on time," Enrico Catalina asked. "Any problems?"

Miguel reached into his shirt pocket, pulling out a joint. He lit it up, inhaling deeply. Miguel blew the smoke out of his nose, "No. No problems, and no one left to tell any tales."

Enrico handed Miguel a brick of bills, then returned to the jet.

The truck was emptied swiftly, with the men on site taking care of the loading. The men secured the hatches, got into an SUV, and left the site. After finishing the last of his joint, Miguel climbed back into the cab. He turned his truck around, pulling to a stop by officer Max.

Miguel rolled the window down, "Same time next week?" He reached for a thick envelope of bills, then tossed it down to the police officer. "For your prompt service!"

The truck and highway patrol car parted ways, driving away just as the three planes took off, disappearing into the night.

**DEA**

The two DEA agents were parked near the highway, surveying the transfer and the planes' loading., using a low-light digital camera to record the faces of the men involved. On the dashboard lay four empty taco wrappers, two pairs of aviator sunglasses, and an incident report of a fire with a photo of burnt bodies: of the dead rancher and his family.

The agents said nothing as they watched the three twin-engine planes take off and the vehicles leave: the SUV, the dual axle truck, and the highway patrol car. They pulled their unmarked SUV onto the road, driving off just as the sun began its journey above the horizon. A lone jackrabbit scampered off to the east, chased by a coyote.

## Ministry of Industrialization, Beijing, China

Pepper grains floated into the candle. General Chen's gaze under his thick graying eyebrows was fixed on the candle's flame atop his desk, next to a photo of a younger him with Chairman Mao. His cigarette smoke curled under his desk lamp. The lamp painted the General in strange shadows in the red hue of the room. There were other pictures of him on the walls, photos of Chen with Ho Chi Min and Chen with Sergei Marcov hung in his darkened office at the Ministry of Industrialization in Beijing.

The sound of rain pelting mercilessly on the windows was distracting. Chen reached out to press the button on the intercom, "Get Legend and Sergei on the phone for the call."

He reminisced as he waited for the inevitable delays of intercontinental communications.

**Laos Border of Vietnam, 1969**

Thirty years earlier in Laos, Chen remembered sitting in the deepest recesses of a Viet Cong tunnel with his fingers dusting gunpowder over a lonely candle on a rickety, small wooden table in the tunnel command center, a Russian AK-47 leaned against the tunnel wall at the ready. The ground shook with explosions above him. As flecks of gunpowder fell on the small flame they randomly sparked. Chen found it hypnotic.

The war raged, topside. The tunnel echoed with the sound of a massive explosion that could only result from a bomb detonating overhead. The tunnel shook, the earth collapsing about him. Chen lay buried beneath the dirt. Only his hand gripping the rifle was visible from the pile of rubble.

**Chen's Office**

General Chen continued gazing at the flame in the expansive red paneled dark room at the Ministry of Industrialization in China. As his aide's voice crackled through the intercom, he snapped out of his reverie.

"Sergei Marcov is on line four," the aide reported.

Chen shuddered, snapping out of his trance. His eyes focused on the phone, his senses returning.

"Chen," the Russian's voice crackled through the phone, "How are the factory plans going?"

The Chinese General's voice had a hard edge: "I will be happier when the final plans are in your hands, Sergei."

Sergei Marcov sat on his bed. The phone pressed to his ear as he listened to the General. His room was surprisingly small for a luxury hotel but tastefully decorated. The artworks on the walls were Salvatore Dali reproductions. On the writing table lay an open Daytimer notebook, a Rolex, and a 9mm pistol. An ice bucket with a bottle of vodka sat next to the weapon. The ashtray needed emptying.

"Is my delivery ready?" he asked.

"Yes," came the clipped answer.

"And is mine. I have a seaplane ready at the Yacht club at nine to meet your fishing trawler at ten."

The Russian turned the disk over in his hands, studying it briefly. He slid it into the laptop case in his lap.

"I have it all scheduled, Chen, and it is all coming together," he could not keep the satisfaction from his voice. "As we foresaw."

"I understand your hackers cost the US Military two hundred million dollars yearly," Chen mused. "After concluding this project, the politburo wants my report on duplicating your cyberwarfare approach."

"I will see you this evening after my plane lands," Chen said.

# Echo Summit

Blinding white snow covered the Tahoe Basin and the rugged mountain pass leading to the city. The jagged edges of each peak shouldered through the entrenchment of deep snow. Cabins dotted the ridgeline of the mountains; the highway below was snowbound. In the distance, a cannon shell's throaty report echoed through the valley. The blast wave of the shell's concussion freed the drifts above the road, and rivers of snow tumbled down across the roadway.

Shortly, another shell exploded above the ridge's crest, adding thunderously to an avalanche roaring down the cliffside.

A nearby Snowplow's radio crackled to life, "All clear."

A fleet of snowplows were standing by. The drivers all fired their engines, gearing up and getting to work at once. The plows had to clear Highway 50 of the twenty-foot wall of snow. Caltrans maintenance workers had learned over the decades that the engine running Tahoe resorts was year-round access.

**Mike Murphy**

Among the cabins looking over Tahoe from the mountains, a brown-haired man, tall with a linebacker's build and in his mid-fifties, stopped mid-shovel. He had been clearing deep snow off the deck of one of the cabins. He heard the cannon and came out onto the deck to enjoy the seasonal spectacle below as an avalanche tore down the cliffside. A long, shallow scar ran across his right cheek, disappearing into the hairline above his ear. A dainty silver locket hung from his neck. The man tucked it into his sweatshirt, smiling at the barrage below the cliff.

Mike Murphy grinned at the chaos before him, "What a show!"

He returned to shoveling the snow once the valley descended into silence again. When he finished, Mike replaced the shovel inside his cabin, returning with a large tripod and field binoculars. It was time to set up his watch post.

## HP Conference Room, Mountain View

"Away from the interruptions all too common in the high-tech industry, we help you manage the productivity of your key employees," John continued. The floor in the conference room at HP was his. He felt confident. "With the conference center so close to HP's workforce, wouldn't you like the assurance that your employees remained focused on your events and be productive?"

Jane White nodded, "You've got my attention, John."

Jane was an attractive woman in her forties. She was a petite, natural blonde, her hair styled in a dramatic cut that framed her features. Her powder blue business suit covered a white silk blouse. "May I call you John?"

"Please do."

"It's not often I ask for more information." Jane unclasped her hands and leaned forward, "I see your laptop. Do you have a presentation for your company for me? Let us see it."

John nodded, relieved that things were going the way he had wanted. "I do indeed. I have our presentation on DVD, and I will leave it with you if you feel anyone else needs to see it." He paused then, checking the flaps of his laptop bag. John looked up sheepishly, "I have the wrong disc with me. I will have to drop one off this afternoon for you."

John felt slightly frazzled. Shaking his head, he opened PowerPoint on his laptop. He pulled down his last file, 99 Presentation.' His computer made a sound.

A prompt popped up on the screen: *NO FILE FOUND.*

He bit the inside of his cheek, opening the CD drive files that read "IIIFabplan."

**Aquatic Park, Berkeley**

The morning sky was clear as Peter ran through the mile-long par trail of the Berkeley Aquatic Park alongside Highway 80. He wore a black tracksuit with red trim. Peter started slowing down, stopping at the push-up station. He grabbed the low pipe above the wet earth, still drenched from the previous day's deluge. He did his usual fifty pushups, breathing heavily during the final ten.

Peter Holland was cooling down, stretching from his par course circuit on a post, when his phone rang.

"Peter here."

"This is George Camper; I am heading to Sacramento to testify at the Capitol today. Do you want to ride up with me for a long interview?"

"Sure, sounds great!"

"I can use the company," George said.

"It will be a long day and a dinner with my aunt. Happy will be there. I recall that you mentioned living in East Bay. How about I pick you up at the Ashby BART Station?"

Peter nodded, excited at the opportunity. "That would be perfect!"

"See you there at 9:30."

The call ended, and Peter was about to tuck it back in the pocket of his tracksuit when it rang again.

"Pete here," he rolled his eyes at the voice on the other end. "Hi, Jean; I cannot talk today; I am heading to Sacramento for an interview. I will call you later tonight. Okay." Peter grabbed his towel and keys and walked to his car.

**Echo Summit**

The large field binoculars mounted on a professional tripod commanded the view of the valley. You could almost make out the aircraft identifications on the runway from this location. Mike Murphy, an FBI Special Agent, was tracing the drug trade used to obtain stolen chipsets in Silicon Valley.

The FBI worked with the DEA on the Silicon Valley cocaine and meth for chips trade. The fact that national security and industrial espionage were being compromised by addicted programmers and line workers lacking sleep in chip fabrication facilities got the attention of both agency heads. The *Upside* reporter behind the exposé would not reveal his sources, but a little leg work brought Mike here to this location today. Mike's cell phone rang.

Agent Pierce dialed his phone from the passenger seat of his SUV.

"Mike? I am Pierce, F.B.I.," he introduced himself. "Do you remember Jorge Esparante?"

"How can I forget him?" Mike said. "He murdered my sister, her family, and my dog, Hoss."

Pierce knew that already, but he needed Mike in on this.

"Why do you ask?" Mike said.

**Four Years Earlier – San Francisco**

Phillip Masters was a slightly overweight, balding, middle-aged banker. His horn-rimmed glasses sat low on the bridge of his nose. He looked at a cute family picture on his desk with a silver locket draped on the frame. His desk phone started ringing.

"Masters," he answered.

Mike Murphy was on the other end, "How's my sister doing, Phillip?"

"Hey, Mike," he leaned back in his chair. "The kids keep her busy. Do not be a stranger. Come over for dinner."

"What about lunch? I am looking into something and need your help," Mike said.

They met at an Asian Fusion restaurant on Mission named Roy's Restaurant. The restaurant's white tablecloths contrasted with the red-backed chairs. Beige paneled walls surrounded the dining area, with a massive wood-framed wine vault behind glass fronts that anchored the restaurant's corner. Asian-themed red, gold, and blue colored art pieces hung on the walls. Mike and Phillip set down their menus and waved over a waiter to take their order.

"It will be right out," the waiter said, taking their menus.

Phillip waited for the waiter to be out of earshot. "How can I help my brother-in-law and the FBI?"

Mike got straight to the point. "Is your bank tied up with the BCCI?"

Phillip straightened up, the friendly smile leaving his face instantaneously. He took off his glasses, lips pressed into a thin line.

Mike met his gaze evenly. "Level with me, Phillip. It is important."

Phillip squirmed where he sat, sweat beading on his forehead. He tugged at his collar, unaware of how quickly the color left his face.

"I don't know where to start," he stuttered.

"How about the beginning?"

Phillip sighed, leaning back for a moment. "A Bahamian bank calls. They need a local bank for a flower import company. Their client was setting up international operations at Mather Field in Sacramento. Jorge Esparante was named as the Columbian importer for the flower distributor." Phillip gathered his thoughts before going on.

"My bank was dealing with the construction sector's hyper-depression hangover, and the extra flow from the flower operations helped the bottom line. It turned out to be a laundering operation, and they keep upping the amounts I must transact."

Mike watched his brother-in-law's face silently.

"They threatened Sally and the kids," he gestured helplessly with his hands.

Mike nodded. "Phillip, I am going to look at their operations. They are importing more than flowers."

The fear on Phil's face was unmistakable.

"Phil, it'll work out, promise." Mike said solemnly, patting Phillip's arm.

### Mather Field, Rancho Cordova

The following night, large racks of flower containers covered the cavernous hangar floor at the Mather Field hangar. Four men extracted bundles of cocaine from the huge shipment.

A UPS plane taxied up the tarmac for the flowers' US distribution. Mike and an FBI team entered the hangar as the shipping operation continued. Mayhem ensued as one of the armed security guards spotted the team, drew his weapon, and fired, hitting an agent. The guard fired again, the bullet grazing Mike's cheek as he took cover. Mike pulled out his service weapon and shot the guard center mass. Two more guards dropped their weapons, then raised their hands in surrender as the first guard hit the floor.

Murphy's team recovered ten thousand kilos of cocaine wrapped in the raid. The DEA photographer took pictures of the agents, the drug haul, and the seized weapons arrayed on the floor.

In his hotel room later that night, Mike woke to his cell phone ringing. He sat up on the edge of the bed, turning on the side table lamp as he rubbed his eyes.

"Murphy." His voice was hoarse.

"I have sad news for you, Mike. Your sister is no longer with us. You better forget about me, or you will see your wife and two kids die soon. Then, I will cut your balls off and feed them to you," hissed the man on the other end of the phone. He knew it was Jorge Esparante. The thick accent gave him away.

Mike was on the edge of the bed, the phone to his ear, his heart thundering.

Later that night, Mike would arrive at the crime scene where the charred bodies of Sally Master, Phillip and their children lay on their elegant living room floor. The Persian rug was charred and unrecognizable from the extinguished fire. Mike's dog, Hoss, lay dead not far off.

Since that fateful night, Mike Murphy had a score to settle. He had yet to catch up to Esparante, but he would. Soon, he thought to himself.

## Present Day

Mike wore Sally's silver locket around his neck as a private jet echoing through the mountain pass brought Mike back to the present.

Pierce's voice broke through the engine noise on Mike's cellphone, "This shipment we're tracking…" he trailed off.

"Is Esparante part of this shipment?" Mike aske, his voice betraying the hatred he felt for the man.

"Yes, we're fairly certain" Pierce said. "We found a rancher and his family dead and burned in El Indio."

## State Capitol

The Senate Committee room chamber was a formal hearing room found in the historic part of the State Capitol Building. A significant historical New Deal work of art backed the dais. It formally hung in the State Courthouse in Los Angeles and found its way north when this facility was renovated in the early 1990s. The commerce committee typically met in committee room 3191 and was moved to room 4203 for the capacity crowd expected for this day's testimony.

Pete arrived early and got a seat at one of the reserved press positions. He plugged his handheld tape recorder into the waiting press feed and settled in. The senate staff made the needed lighting and camera adjustments for the CalSpan broadcast. Integrating the broadcast cameras on the wall on either side of the massive painting was a tricky engineering feat. The Sergeants-at-Arms of the Senate were in position, and the technicians finished the audiovisual system's final settings.

A staffer in a beige suit carefully moved behind the overstuffed leather chairs at the dais, her arms overflowing with the one hundred-page reports she placed next to the senators' positions.

**HP Conference Room**

"I am sorry this took so long, Ms. White," John apologized.

"Jane, please," she said politely. "That's all right, but now I wonder how technically solid your conference center is, John?"

John reddened under the teasing.

"What happened?" he said sheepishly, "A customer must have taken the disc yesterday morning. I was supporting a last-minute teleconference and had to get to lunch. It was my girlfriend's birthday, now-fiancée. The customer must have mistakenly taken my disc; they were identical looking."

"Congratulations, John! I have heard excellent things about your conference center," Jane said good-naturedly, "I want a copy dropped off by tomorrow morning, I have a weekly lunch meeting with our Operations VP, and he should see it."

"I will drop it off before lunch. Thank you so much." John stood, fighting hard to keep his embarrassment at bay.

"Thank you for coming in. I am looking forward to our development meeting next month at your facility. Good-bye."

John shook her hand and left her office, satisfied with the meeting despite the little bump.

**Echo Summit**

Esparante's Lear Jet streaked near Echo Summit while lining up the mile-high airport runway from Luther Pass over Highway 89. The numbers were readable on the tail. Fifteen hundred feet below, the Upper Truckee River flows toward Lake Tahoe, six miles south of the runway. Mike watched as the Lear Jet descended through the valley to a landing, then taxied to its hangar.

## Seaplane

The sky was clear, the air cold and crisp, and Jim Fowler was on his latest flight for this client. He picked up a used 1957 HU-16E Albatross flying boat for its long-range speed and a service ceiling of twenty-one thousand feet for under $400,000. One of 466 built and cheap enough he could abandon if necessary. The two 1,425 HP Cyclone R-1820-76A radial piston engines clawed the plane into the air, leaving a grasp of the swells below.

He had just met the client's vessel off the North Coast of California one hundred miles at sea. Fowler learned his trade like many of his peers. He was one of those Air America pilots who flew in supplies, in that secret little war in Laos, during the Vietnam War.

The CIA brokered support from the Hmong, the hill tribes, by shipping weapons, money, and rice. They had empty planes, and taking off the short runways hacked into the jungle-covered mountains was manageable. Their beneficiaries started asking them to take family, pigs, and chickens to sell to the US troops in Da Nang. Not much later those planes were filled with drugs destined for an array of markets on suddenly lengthened runways by the CIA's Warlords.

So, when the conflict ended and the United States' presence wound down in Asia, Jim was suddenly out of work. And he was a little hooked on the excitement and the hazard pay.

A call came from an old airline pilot friend, Barry Seal, who was now working for a small start-up operation in Columbia. The following week, Jim was flying his first seaplane load out of Cartagena.

Some twenty years later, he was still flying. These days, he is much choosier about his clients. He liked working for the well-connected, those with the juice to secure the landing zones. You never knew whom you would be working for next in this business. He was retired but was drawn back for a great offer by an old name he knew from 1965. He advised on new routes, airports, and the latest flight plans that raised the fewest flags. He reckoned six more flights and he would be on a year-round vacation in Puerto Vallarta. He could almost taste that salty margarita now.

**South Lake Tahoe Airport**

The Lear Jet's engines wound down as two vehicles met the plane. One was a hotel limousine that transferred the pilots' baggage, and the other was a hotel van. Two cargo men emptied the jet's hold, and other luggage from the plane.

The pilots and Enrico Catalina promptly left the airport. The van stayed to receive the rest of the plane's cargo.

## Chase Plane

The blue team's chase plane was five miles away, keeping the chance of detection small. Using high-powered binoculars, the team leader radioed Mike to move up. Two loaded vehicles were moving, and Mike needed to cover the airport and the loop road.

## Foster City

Later that morning, John pulled into the Crown Plaza parking lot. He found his site manager at the hotel—an Australian ex-pat named Stephen. He was a wizard at running live events and was an ex-roadie for many San Francisco bands like Eddie Money, Montrose, and Greg Kihn.

John nodded at him as he approached, "Yo, Stephen."

The ex-pat glanced up, looking slightly disheveled, "Yo, John!"

John raised his eyebrows, taking in Stephen's sallow skin and the dark circles under his eyes. He looked in a rough shape. "What truck drove over you last night? I have seen you look better after a twenty-week tour."

Stephen snorted, "Some mates of mine are in from Australia," he ran a hand through his hair. "After the Oracle event, we got a little twisted. I might have to admit I'm getting too old for all-nighters, John."

"I will get one of those walkers on order for you." John thumped him on the shoulder in mock sympathy.

"How's Laura?" Stephen asked, ignoring the jibe. "She is one great gal."

John smiled, "Glad you think so," struggling to keep his expression neutral as he said, "Now I can invite you to the wedding."

The smile on Steven's face showed his surprise and joy, "About time you made her legal. A girl like that could get you arrested in the company of an old fart like yourself."

"That's the kettle calling the pot black, bro."

"Did you hear about Jim's uncle Larry's passing?"

"Jim Kelly? No!" John shook his head in shock. "Is he still here?"

"He's in the ballroom," Stephen gestured, "finishing the loadout."

John went to the Crown Plaza's ballroom to find his friend. Jim Kelly was in the room's far corner, disassembling a fast-fold rear projection screen. Walking over to him, John put a hand on Jim's shoulder.

"Sorry to hear about Larry," he offered. "What happened?"

"Thanks; he had a massive heart attack chasing a bank robber in downtown Oakland," Jim explained, glancing up at John and shaking John's offered hand. "The service is on Saturday at Mountain View Cemetery in Piedmont. Half of the force will be in attendance."

"I will never forget the playoff tickets he treated us to for the Raiders. I wish I could make it," he said. "I promised Laura a weekend in Santa Cruz to celebrate our engagement."

Jim rose to his feet, smiling. "Way to go, John!" he clapped him on his back.

"Please let Sue know she's in my prayers."

**Echo Summit**

Mike had tracked the Lear pilot's skillful descent flaring onto the runway. He stood, keying his radio as he gathered his gear, "Heads up, they are on the ground. Give them plenty of room."

Mike tossed his gear into his SUV. He pulled out of the driveway and made a sharp left at the Echo Summit Lodge onto the Lincoln Highway. The FBI agent drove down the switchback to Highway 50, which was finally clear. He stepped on the gas.

**Emerald Bay**

The Albatross flying boat landed at Emerald Bay. The plane passed Fannette Island; the stone shell of a dilapidated tea house jutted out of the snow on top of the island. Emerald Bay was shrouded in deep snowdrifts, and the water was mirror-smooth, except for the wake of the plane's pontoons. The pilot tied the plane to a dock on the bay's western end.

The side hatch opened on Sergei Marcov. He climbed down the passenger ladder, then helped the two Chinese passengers, Lin Lee, and her brother Kai, disembark the seaplane. The pilot pulled a large briefcase from the cargo bay and secured the door.

The group walked to the secluded resort Vikingsholm, following a path cleared from the dock to the resort through large drifts of snow. Sergei offered his arm to steady Lin, then smiled at her. She was a beauty.

"I trust the flight was not too bumpy?" he asked.

"When do we see older brother?" she asked in a troubled voice.

Sergei smiled, patting her arm reassuringly. "Tonight, my dear, tonight. After tonight, you will never miss seeing him again." He promised.

## South Lake Tahoe

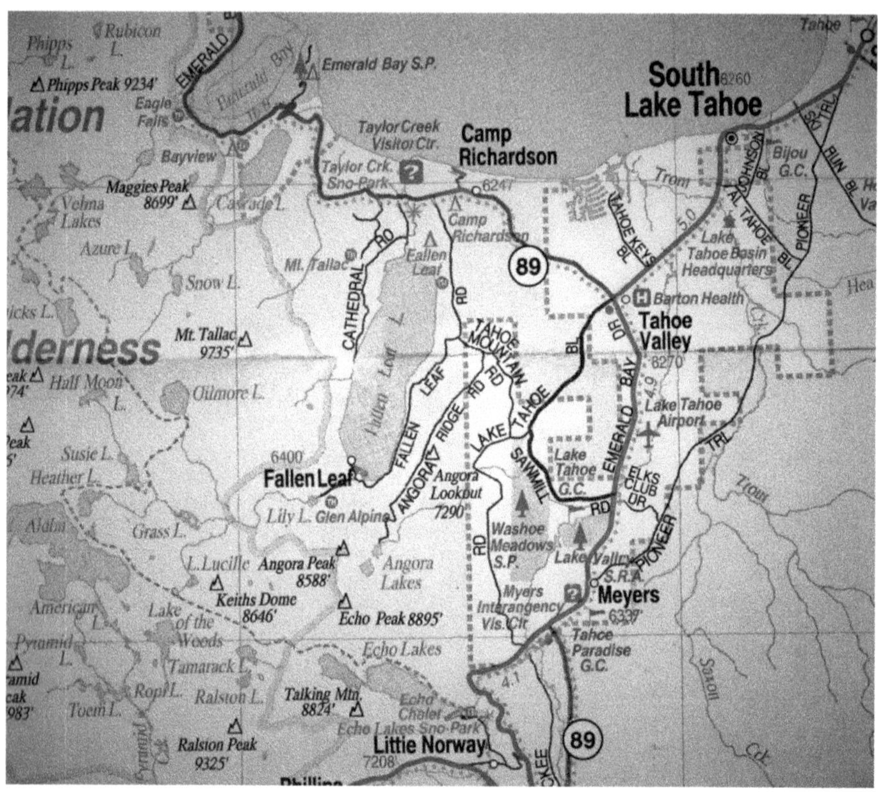


The limo and van both exited the airport, turning right onto Highway 50, and followed the highway as it turned east toward the casinos.

40-year-old Agent Taylor lowered his binoculars in a powder-blue ski parka, placing his half-eaten Big Mac onto the center console. He keyed his radio.

"Mike, we have a Harrah's black van and a limo on 50 heading toward Stateline," he reported.

Taylor stuffed the remains of the Big Mac into his mouth and put on his sunglasses, wheeling his SUV onto the highway, swerving across the road to the right-hand lane, cutting off a car in the process.

Mike keyed his radio, "I am behind you half a click. Do not crowd them."

Mike overtook a Subaru with a ski rack.

"I lost the van. It must have turned off on Tahoe Keys Boulevard." Agent Taylor's voice crackled through the radio.

"I have Tahoe Keys. You keep going." Mike ordered.

Mike turned on Lake Tahoe Boulevard and signaled a left turn onto Tahoe Keys Road. He accelerated down the plowed road with four-foot snow shoulders, navigating his car smoothly along the sweeping right turn.

He looked to his left, noticing fresh tire tracks entering Capri Drive, yanking the steering wheel too hard. The car oversteered on the turn, Mike fought the skid and raced down the road, hot on the new trail.

The tracks turned left onto the last street. Mike slowed his truck down in time to see a man leaving Harrah's van at the end of the road. The man rushed around the side of the home on the cul-de-sac. Mike spotted the driver still in the vehicle.

He stared down the street, parking his truck as he reached for his radio handset.

"I need to re-task Tango Charlie Five to the Tahoe Keys. I need eyes on the end of Beach Drive, and I cannot get any closer."

A heavy-set, bald, thick-necked man in a black ski jacket walked rapidly around the side of a home. He pulled a black knit cap out of his pocket and tugged it over his massive head. The hat covered a large burn scar. He was laboring, breathing hard as he trekked through the deep snowfall.

He rounded the back of the house, grabbed a snow shovel, and briskly strode onto the private dock. He first muscled through four feet of snow engulfing the pier, then attacked the boat cover. Using his arms with wide swings, he pushed the powdery snow into the water to clear the purchase of the edges of the surface. After storing the shell in a hatch, he dropped to one knee, untying the white, 51-foot Sea Ray 510 Cabin Cruiser. The man climbed aboard.

As he started the boat, the motor rumbled. He piloted the cruiser out of the dock and around the jetty, then motored onto the smooth, glassy water.

**State Capitol**

In Senate room #4203, George Camper entered the hearing room in a navy blue, double-breasted suit. The Sergeant-at-Arms showed him his chair. His red and blue tie and white collared blue shirt set off with an American flag pin on the lapel of his pin-striped suit. James Tate, a distinguished older senator chairing the hearing, pounded the gavel.

"I call this hearing to order." Tate's voice boomed. "I have a few comments before I give the floor to Mr. Camper for his opening remarks. This committee is conducting a regional fact-finding hearing to explore the scope of physical and electronic security required for our technology companies and communications systems. We will be exploring the Russian and Chinese cyberthreats to our national security..."

After the senator's opening remarks, Senator Tate begins the hearing by introducing George Camper. All eyes were on Camper. He leaned forward, pressing the talk button on the gooseneck microphone base.

"Senators, I am here to deliver unbelievably bad news. My team has discovered severe flaws in the Windows operating system, an operating system used throughout Washington, D.C. that leaves us and all our government's secrets vulnerable to attack from outside...entities." His voice was grave, his expression serious. "Last year's approval by NHS to release of crucial satellite launch guidance details to China has only increased their ability to penetrate our industrial and military secrets. Additionally, I must mention the industrial theft and espionage by the heavy trade in cocaine and meth in our high technology industries."

**Lake Tahoe**

The pursuit plane, Tango Charlie Five, is a twin-engine Cessna. The pilot had a 360° view of the entire Tahoe Basin flying at five thousand feet above the lake. The region is laden white with the recent deep snowfall. The lack of trees suggested the ski runs of Heavenly Valley. Below was the wake of the cabin cruiser TC-5 was following. The pilot watched through a pair of binoculars.

Mike glanced at the map unfurled over his SUV's steering wheel and dashboard.

"Mike, I've got your cabin cruiser leaving the marina," TC-5's pilot radioed in. "Heading northwest. Looks like they are in a hurry."

"I'll find a side street and settle in," Mike responded.

**Emerald Bay**

Emerald Bay's hillsides were covered by four feet of recent snow. The cabin cruiser motored into Emerald Bay, passing Fannette Island. Nearing the dock, the boat was throttled back, the bow settling into the water, gliding into the berth next to the seaplane.

The boat captain tossed a line to the pilot waiting on the pier. The pilot and captain shook hands. Sergei Markov walked down the pier to meet the two men. Sergei was in an expansive mood, cheerful because this first deadline had been met.

"Good timing," the Russian commented. "I trust the cargo is intact."

"I have a thousand kilos in the van," Dimitri answered flatly.

"Here's my part of the deal," Sergei said, handing Jim a felt sack.

Jim peered into it, examining the contents. He pulled the drawstring closed again, tossed the felt sack in his flight case, and gave Sergei a thumbs up.

"Let me get their luggage. Dimitri, can you give me a hand?" Jim pulled two suitcases from the cabin, handing them to Dimitri.

Jim took his seat behind the controls and started the seaplane's engine.

Waiting at the end of the pier were Kai Lee and his sister Lin Lee who had arrived with Sergei. He motioned them to approach, then helped both find safe seating in the cruiser cabin. Sergei sat down next to Lin. Kai was unhappy at Sergei's eager attention to his younger sister, and hoped this business would be completed by the end of the week.

Dimitri backed away from the dock, slowly increasing speed toward the mouth of the bay just as the seaplane lifted off the water, soon soaring overhead, rocking its wings. Sergei watched the plane go with a big smile on his face. Phase one complete.

**South Lake Tahoe**

Mike waited in his truck, leaning back in his seat, one foot propped up on the dash, watching the sun sparkle on the water.

"Heads up, Mike. They made a delivery and pick-up," TC-5's pilot radioed. "They are coming back at you with at least four on board. A seaplane just lifted off; I must follow. Sorry, we are short of air support—everything is snowbound."

"Chase Three," Mike keyed his radio. "I'm going to need some help."

**State Capitol**

In the Committee room, George Camper leaned into his microphone again.

"Senator, I'm afraid I can't discuss that topic in a public forum due to its classified nature."

A young, petite, attractive brunette aide in a dark green suit squeezed behind the senators to place a note in front of Chairman Tate. The aide and Chairman discussed the message off the microphone.

"Mr. Camper, thank you for your insightful words regarding our national security," the senator said. "I hope you have time for an informal meeting with the Governor and me after we close the hearing?"

George Camper smiled, "I would be delighted to make myself available."

**Tahoe Keys Beach Drive**

The cabin cruiser reduced speed to under five knots as it entered the jetty and docks of the Capri Drive rental. Dimitri tied down the boat as stood at the stern. Lin tentatively grasped Dimitri's hand and gingerly stepped onto the snow-encrusted dock. The four had difficulties trudging through the deep snow to enter the rear of the house. Sergei's expression was severe, his displeasure at trudging through the snow, clear.

"Sorry, Boss," Dimitri said. "I didn't have time to clear the snow off and meet the plane on time."

"The snow won't kill them," Sergei Marcov commented.

Dimitri laughed deeply and continued in Russian, "That is funny."

They reached the covered back porch and stomped off the snow from the waist down.

Moments later, the garage door opened, and a black Mercedes S600 pulled out onto the heated snow-free driveway. The van backed in alongside the limo. The driver got out and moved to the van's rear, opening its doors, and transferring duffel bags to the trunk of the Mercedes. Dimitri added the two suitcases he carried from the boat and closed the lid.

"Give this to Enrico at the hotel." Sergei handed a thin package to the driver. "And thank him."

Dimitri opened the door for Sergei and the Chens. The driver entered the van and drove away. The Mercedes followed behind as they turned onto Capri Drive.

Mike watched Harrah's Shuttle Van drove by, followed closely by the Mercedes S600.

"Chase Three, there are two vehicles on the move. Take the Shuttle Van, and I will follow the Mercedes," Mike radioed.

Mike waited, tapping his fingers on the steering wheel. After a minute, he gradually pulled his car out from the side street and followed the limo, his slow pace.

"Mike, the van is heading east, and the limo is heading west, on 50," Chase Three reported over the radio.

Mike accelerated down the road to Highway 50. He braked hard, making a right turn. He punched the gas, heading off in pursuit. Mike could not see the Mercedes at the junction of highways. He followed the traffic west on fifty. Mike passed a snowplow clearing the shoulder.

**Highway 50**

The Mercedes cleared the agricultural inspection station and passed a fuel truck climbing to Echo Summit. Mike's SUV approached the Inspection Checkpoint. He pulled out his wallet, flashing his badge as he passed the officer. He spotted the limousine further up the hill behind a tourist bus. Mike trailed behind the fuel truck at an agonizing pace.

In the limo, Dimitri turned his head to the rear and spoke to Sergei in Russian, "Boss, I'm not sure, but we might have picked up a tail."

Sergei looked over his shoulder and down the road. He turned back and leaned forward, "Pass this bus and make some mischief, Dimitri."

Dimitri grinned, "No worries, Boss."

The Mercedes was behind the bus, and as the road carved around the hillside, the limo quickly overtook the bus. The climbing lane ended when Dimitri fishtailed the limo into the rear of an SUV going the other way, setting off a chain reaction of crashes and closing the roadway. The limo returned to its lane just as a CalTrans truck collided with the bus.

Sergei glanced in the rearview mirror, the ghost of a smile on his face as he took in the turbulence left in their wake. Lin Lee screamed in shock.

"Well done, Dimitri," Sergei said in English. "Ms. Lee, I cannot allow anyone to follow you. You want to be with your long-missed brother, yes?"

Mike had been making a dangerous pass of the fuel truck where the slow truck lane ended. Mike's eyes widened as he spotted the traffic pile up ahead before he could return to his side of the road. The fuel truck had started jackknifing its trailer into Mike's car. He gritted his teeth and, stomping on the gas, he turned the wheel hard, aiming for the same road he came down this morning.

Mike's car spun three hundred and sixty degrees as the tanker and the CalTrans truck collided, the gas load exploding into a massive fireball beside him.

Mike grunted, fear and anger mixed as he steered into the slide and added power to the wheels.

Mike guided his SUV around the two hairpin turns to switch back up the cliff with snow rooster trails from the wheels. At the top of the ridge, the truck lost traction, and the rear end spun out to the left as it passed the Echo Summit Lodge, barely missing a small snowplow working in the parking lot.

Mike passed a sign for Echo Lakes and Camp Harvey West as the truck raced downhill. It sparked his memory of being a Boy Scout at Camp Harvey West on Upper Echo Lake. The one merit badge he always remembers was the mile swim in upper Echo Lake's frigid waters. On the day of his swim, the water temperature was 54 degrees. The hour and ten minutes were an all-out swim.

Mike's SUV reached Highway 50 on ramp, picking up speed as the highway continued downhill. Mike's shoulders relaxed as he loosened his tight grip on the wheel. His face eased. Mike keyed the microphone.

"The limo caused a wreck on Echo Summit," he reported, "Highway 50 is closed to all traffic for the next several hours. Call ahead to Sacramento and get me help. I am ahead of the limo and will let them pass me in ten miles."

# California State Capitol

Warren, the Sergeant at Arms, kept a close eye on the public. Right behind him, Peter had a front seat in the press section and was within ear-shot of Camper as the hearing ended. The US and California State Senators invited them to the hearing huddled with George Camper for the new transaction/ID standard details. Peter could hear the majority of what they said to each other. Heated discussions continued outside in the corridors of the second-floor hearing room.

"Well, it supports native Java code, and Microsoft, to license, has to support the code." With Sun suing Microsoft for Java code violations, George knew he could take advantage of the situation. "We will audit Microsoft's code to assure our investors' investments," finished George.

"Gentlemen, the Governor would like to speak with you before you leave," the Sergeant at Arms broke in.

"Well, I promised the Governor. I will see you in Washington next week, gentlemen." Camper said, nodding at the men around him in farewell. "Thank you for your interest in helping small businesses compete safely worldwide."

"Thank you, Mr. Camper, for coming on such short notice. My staff send their regards to your aunt. I hear she is doing well after the fall and hip surgery," added the State Senator, Roland Carpenter.

"Thank you, for your interest. "My Aunt Em is one tough bird," George shook Roland's hand. "Have a safe trip, Senator."

Camper gathered Peter, busy with position statements, for his three-part article in *Upside*.

**Mike on Highway 50**

Mike's focus returned to driving on Highway 50. He was ahead of the S600. He accelerated the SUV, passing Camp Sacramento, and continued down Highway 50 past Horsetail Falls. He parked his car in

Kyburz, behind Strawberry Lodge. The Mercedes 600 came along two minutes later with no traffic behind them. He waited, giving them miles of room. Mike pulled out and paced the limo.

"Blue Goose, come in," Mike said as he raced down the hill toward Sacramento.

"Romeo 6 where are you?" came the response.

"Highway 50 just left Kyburz, and the Mercedes is down the road two miles; I could use some help," Mike reported.

"How did you get over the summit with the accident those bastards created?" Tim commented, doing nothing to hide his disbelief.

"The road is closed; it will be hours before they clear it. So, no help for you on the ground, I am afraid. And do you want to hear the good or bad news?" Another voice crackled over the radio.

"Always the bad news first because it always gets better," answered Mike.

"Bad news is that you have no air support. The seaplane is still in the air."

"Okay, now what's the good news?" Mike knew where this was going.

**Governor's Office**

Senator Graham and George Camper sat in the governor's outer office on a plush couch.

"The May Five Committee Report found technical information transferred during the last campaign enables the Peoples' Republic of China to improve its present and future space launch vehicles and ICBMs," Graham said. "It was part of the Johnny Chung, Loral, and Clinton 1996 fundraising mess."

"Cisco, Intel, and IBM have contacted the FBI about their employees' trading microprocessors and trade secrets for drugs." George Camper told the senator. "We worry about backdoors written into operating systems by compromised programmers. Did you know the Pentagon spends over two hundred million dollars in counter-cyber warfare this year alone?"

Just then, the governor's aide opened the inner office door. The aide wore a red power suit; she was a petite, fortyish blonde, "The Governor will be with you in a few minutes; he's just finishing up with the Prison Guard Union."

**Mike's SUV**

"The good news is that we have no additional resources to go over budget," Tim said in his Mississippi drawl. "As you are on the road and we cannot get any cars to you, Sacramento will have to provide another two cars, and, as we do not have enough planes to cover the two that came in. I will see if the Highway Patrol's plane will join in." Tim stopped to take a breath. Mike. listening to the radio, waited for the other shoe to drop.

"But that is a big maybe," Tim continued, "there is a high-speed chase on Highway 5. A nut in a Viper is doing 180, tying up all their planes. Call me if you need anything. Out." Tim had to deal with his problems.

*'Piece of cake,'* Mike thought to himself.

**Capitol Rotunda**

Peter Holland admired a massive, white, Carrara marble statue of Columbus' Last Appeal to Queen Isabella in the center of Rotunda. The white figure sat on the floor of Belgium black, and Vermont white marble tiles arranged in a checkerboard pattern. The second-floor balcony circled the large, domed opening. George Camper walked up to Peter and tapped him on the shoulder.

"Peter, sorry it took so long," he apologized. "The Governor had a few questions for me."

"I took the tour and saw the building restoration cutouts in the basement. I could use a drink." Peter said delightedly, turning to face George.

"You're a mind reader, and we have time before dinner." George looked at his wristwatch, a smile on his face. "Happy can make the dinner. Do you mind watching for her when I get Auntie Em?"

They walked down the corridor, passing the Governor's aide walking in the opposite direction. She stopped typing on her BlackBerry, then reached over to stop George Camper.

"Mr. Camper, I was e-mailing you. The Governor wants you to meet with the Office of Emergency Services and our Public Utilities Commission about the Y2K issue. Is 10 a.m. good for you?" she asked.

George turned to Peter with a questioning look, "Peter, do you mind getting a lift with Happy back to the Bay Area?"

"Sounds like a bribe to get me out of my interview with you," he commented, then shrugged. "Sure. Happy is better-looking than you."

George suppressed a smile and turned back to the aide. "I've cleared my schedule; e-mail me the details."

The aide's attention went back to her phone, though she waved before parting.

"Tell the teachers' union to cool their jets." Peter called the aide. "The prison guards' get a turn this year."

George and Peter grinned at the sausage-making of government. They turned to the north entrance of the Capitol and exited the building.

George grabbed Peter's arm as they left. "I have a suitable place to wash down a jaded political discussion—Frank Fats. Time to make good on the rest of the interview."

They walked down 'L' Street past the State Treasury Building to the bar.

**Frank Fat's**

Legendary restaurateur Frank Fat opened his first restaurant in 1939 in a rundown, former speakeasy two blocks west of the State Capitol. With the $2,000 investment he had borrowed, the restaurant quickly became a favorite among politicians, lobbyists, and government officials. Its widespread popularity earned it its "Third House" nickname because it was the preferred haunt of legislators, governors, and the state's most powerful men and women.

It was a long, narrow bar and restaurant. The red ceiling over the bar vaulted up to a golden Buddha. The back of the bar had a pagoda theme, and a mirror dominated the bar itself.

George and Peter sat in a booth across from the end of the long bar. The dark bar was bathed in light when a patron opened the entry door.

Overweight politicians filled the bar among power-suited lobbyists and abundant attractive females. Conversation snippets echoed across the long room.

"Your teachers did well with the last budget. The Governor must square up with the prison guards this year," warned one politician.

George turned his back to the table and took a long sip before setting down his drink. "Ever heard of Level Three or Google?" he asked Peter.

"I did a story a couple of years ago about Level Three's network operation center in Denver and their overbuilding of dark fiber by five times the possible demand," Peter said.

George took another sip. "We saw that bubble pop in September, didn't we? The network will be everything, and Google will be a big player. Security of the internet is the issue."

George motioned to the waiter in the universal signal to ask for the check. "Drink up. It is time I picked up Aunt Em. She does not move fast, and at 84, she is recovering from hip surgery."

Peter rose with him. "I'm going to drop you at Twenty-Eight on the way over, and I need you to watch for Happy," George said.

As they exited Frank Fat's, George said, "The restaurant we are going to was formerly the Capitol Grill, and it was a very trendy political watering hole. Willie Brown was seen there often during his reign as Assembly Speaker." They turned right to retrieve George's car from the Capitol parking garage beneath the Capitol Building. "The restaurant started the winemaker dinners," George continued, "and when the owner decided to upscale, he kept up with the wineries sponsoring dinners. Tonight, is BV!" Peter kept up with him as they mounted the steps.

"I'm unsure if I am hungrier or need a good glass of wine after the past few days," George added.

"I would say, sir, that you should raise a toast for the great work and a done deal," Peter responded.

"Never say a deal is done before it is. Please take that as fatherly advice. My father once lost three hundred thousand dollars. He just needed the signature on a contract and called the client. The client asked him to come over right away. He was about to play a round of golf. My father told him to have a good game and that he would be over in the morning. The guy died on the golf course of a heart attack an hour later! So never think a deal done until the check clears." George winked at Peter.

Peter arched his brows in surprise at the story.

"By the way," George began conspiratorially, "I think you got my sister's attention."

"She's a fine woman," Peter admitted.

"Well, if we don't get there on time, she can be an impatient one," said George.

The Capitol's gilded elevator employed an operator who took them down to the basement level of the building. The elevator had not been updated to self-serve. That was something Peter really liked about the state Capitol.

Peter and George found his parked Mercedes. George pulled out of the basement garage on the south side of the building and turned left onto 'N' Street. George shifted smartly and caught the light at 15th Street since 'N' Street was closed for road work, and they took 19th over to 'Q' Street.

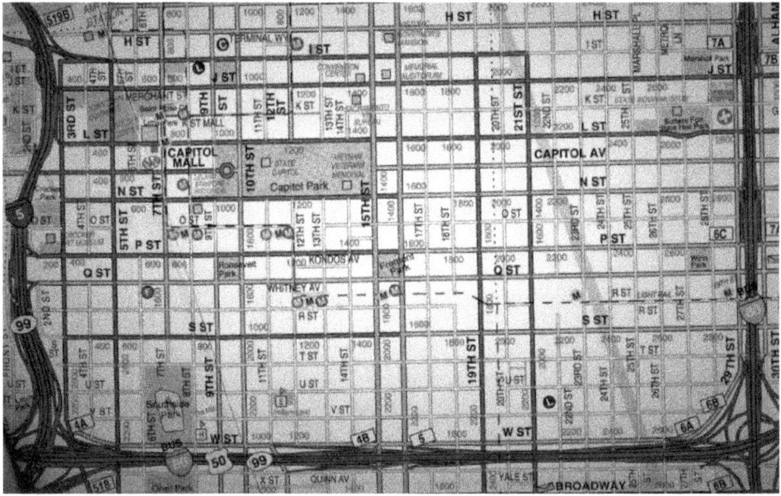

The drive to the Eastern edge of Midtown was short but not without consequence. Two cars ran the stoplight at 16th Street, causing George to brake hard.

At 21st Street, a Sacramento Bee employee blindly crossed the road and was nearly run down by the Mercedes. George had been timing the traffic lights up 'Q' Street, and when the roadway dipped, passing 21st, and there was no way to see the jaywalker. Good thing he had ABS brakes. A car beside theirs skidded to a stop after clipping a parked car. Peter grabbed the dash with both hands to avoid flying into the windshield.

"I am sure she will need to change her underwear when she gets home—that was close," George commented with a grim chuckle as he loosens his grip on the wheel. "It reminds me of the Darwin Awards."

"Darwin Awards?" Peter was intrigued.

"The Darwin Awards are given posthumously to the winners. The last winner's trophy went to two brothers. There was a storm, the power went out, and they smelled a gas leak. The brothers went to the basement to investigate. It was pitch black, and they lit their cigarette lighters for light. They were winners. I should get her name and send it in as the nominee for still living life achievement awards."

"Yesterday, I was driving to an early meeting in the Financial District, an IPO offering from London, before your press conference," Peter began. "I was timing the lights just like now. It was 6 a.m., and the streets were empty. Out of nowhere, a jogger ran out in front of my car. He had his headphones on and did not even look for traffic. I locked up my brakes and slid through the intersection at Montgomery alongside a blue station wagon. The car's skid allowed my front bumper to miss him. I am not even sure if he knew what happened. Can I add my nomination to yours?"

"We're here, Peter." George dropped him off on the corner of 28th and 'N' Streets "Do me a favor— wait here and watch for Happy. She is usually very prompt and does not like waiting." Peter climbed out of the car.

"We will both benefit by you keeping her entertained while I go collect Em."

Kitty corner was a regional transit bus maintenance facility; across 'N' Street, a parking lot, and another restaurant called Paragary's. Peter liked the name and the big windows.

Peter checked in with the hostess at the eatery, and she directed him across the street for a drink. "We will call you when Mr. Camper shows up."

Stepping out into the brisk night air, Peter spotted Happy in a tight, red leather jacket and skirt outfit, carrying a briefcase, entering Paragary's across the street. As Peter stepped off the curb, as a limo turned the corner, the headlights blinded Peter for a second. Peter jumped back and cursed himself for nearly entering the Darwin Awards' final rounds.

### Mike's SUV

Mike watched the limo nearly run down, an idiot stepping off the curb without looking. He looked like a stunned deer in his headlights.

"You got to be careful, mate," he said to himself.

The S600 had just stopped past the valet station and parked. Mike had no choice but to continue to 'O' Street and turn right. John continued around the block, turned right on 27th Street, and killed his lights. Another right turn into the alley brought his car to the parking lot across the street. A Z3 pulled out of the front parking space on the curb on 28th Street, and Mike had a clear view of the limo driver who had just turned around the corner on 'N' Street.

The large Mercedes pulled up alongside the curb. Moments later, a tan Lexus parked on the other side of the road. An Asian man approached the parked Mercedes. Mike had missed the Lexus when it first pulled up. The Asian signaled the Mercedes driver, who powered down the rear windows of the auto. Mike noticed a lady waving her hand at the Asian man. As soon as the woman waved, the window rolled up, and the limousine pulled away from the curb.

The two men spoke animatedly with each other. A few minutes later, Mike spotted the idiot one more time heading back to the site of the recent near roadkill.

**Peter**

Paragary's, an urban eatery with a well-heeled clientele, was crowded that night, and Peter struggled to spot Happy. He stood at the entrance, looking over the tables to find her, but he did not see her. Giving up, he approached the host station.

"Do you have a reservation?" she asked.

Ignoring her question, he inquired, "Did you see where the brunette in red went? She just came in."

"Lucky you!" she replied. "She went into the patio area, sir." The hostess waved her arm toward a door off the far side of the bar.

"Thanks," Peter nodded in acknowledgment and headed toward the patio, passing the long bar on the restaurant's left side. The bar was three deep with an extensive happy hour crowd in conversations and queuing for drinks. He heard snippets of discussions about the 49ers, the weather, and skiing.

Peter entered the patio, pleasantly surprised by the large, enclosed, lushly landscaped area. Casual jazz created the atmosphere as it played softly in the background.

Three waterfalls cascaded from rust-colored, iron sunflowers topping eight-foot-long shoots, anchored in large terra cotta pots.

*The waterfall sound reminded Peter of a time in India. He was out of college and had taken a camera and notepad with him to write about India. After a month of visiting the Utter Pradesh State, he finally returned to New Delhi. He was tired, thirsty, and sick from the noise of countless cars and trucks riding their horns. All the truck owners paint their tailgates in India with 'Horn Please' encouraging the unceasing din.*

*Staying at the Sheraton Hotel; Peter looked forward to the American-style buffet, an oasis of comfort food he could sink his teeth into. The fifty-foot marble-clad walls with water cascading down their surface made the soothing noise that enveloped his senses. He would always remember that sound and the relief of ordinary creature comforts.*

# MILD MANNERED MEN

*It was not that he had a horrible trip. He loved it. He was tired of the tourist hotels he stayed in worldwide; they were all the same. But a month of sponge baths, purifying one's drinking water daily, and meals that were nothing like the Indian restaurants in the States had made him eager for the soothing embrace and quiet. He remembered...*

He finally spotted her.

*It is amazing what a sound can bring back memories,* he thought, going to the bar.

At the outdoor bar, Happy talked to a dark-haired white man in his fifties and an older Asian man. Peter scowled, taking an instant dislike for the Slavic-looking man. He looked too self-confident and, with the deep scar on his cheek, too untrustworthy. Peter's hostility increased as he watched the man playfully flirting with Happy.

The bar had two mirrors with large, seascape-themed frames. Galvanized steel covered the bar and the seating. Peter's gaze found Happy again, and his heartbeat increased slightly. He was getting more interested in Happy than he realized.

Olive trees in large ceramic planters define the outdoor area. A trellis provided a backdrop and allowed for indirect lighting. Peter noted that the space heaters were glowing, fighting the chill for dinners.

As he approached the trio, Peter overheard him say in flawless, accented English, "We have several important steps to complete, and our timetable is running short. I cannot be focused on you until our business is complete."

"I have the finance in place, Sergei. You need to be less stressed about it." Happy replied.

"You need to collaborate with me more on several other projects, Happy," Sergei said as he stroked her shoulder.

Peter found his opening. "Hi, Happy," he greeted. "I saw you walk in." Happy was startled but recovered fast.

She smiled, animated. "Peter!"

Happy's open red leather jacket revealed a sheer, black silk top that matched her black tights, her legs descending from the red leather skirt into four-inch red heels.

"Your brother is picking up your aunt and should be only another twenty minutes," he reported.

"Well, this is a nice surprise," she replied.

Peter turned to face Happy, with his back slightly toward the other two men. Peter eyed the Slavic man, taking in his dark monochrome appearance and the large military ring on his finger. He did not like his intimacy with Happy.

Still distracted and unsure how to address the other man, he said, "Your brother needs to stay another day on business in Sacramento. Would you mind giving me a lift back to the city?" He made eye contact with the Slavic man, "I'm sorry—I'm Peter Holland."

"Sergei Marcov," he introduced himself.

"And I am Lee," followed the Asian man in the powder blue jacket.

"Pleasure to meet both of you," he nodded good-naturedly at each of them as he shook their hands.

"Peter, Sergei is a former member of the Russian Trade Consul," Happy added.

"Pleasure to meet you, Mr. Holland," Sergei responded, heavily accented. "I—we have a matter to finish, Ms. Camper. Excuse us for a moment."

Sergei and Lee took their leave and joined another slightly built Asian man at a table near one of the fountains along the far wall.

"I see I have a rival, Ms. Camper," Peter said, smiling playfully.

Happy chuckled. "Sergei is manly and mysterious—but he is a client. I never mix personally with clients. Even though he insists otherwise."

Peter nodded, his eyes tracking the Russian's movements. Sergei picked up the check, and the three men got up and exited through the patio gate.

"So," Peter thought about how to phrase his question best. "Is it a state secret to ask what deal you are cooking up? *Upside* readers want to know."

Happy arched an eyebrow, her dark eyes giving away nothing. "Peter, we'll get along just fine." Her hand landed on his forearm. "But no prying, okay?"

Peter nodded glibly, "I am yours to command."

Happy's serious expression turned into one of bemusement. "That could get interesting."

Peter felt the warmth of a flush on his cheeks.

A few moments later Sergei returned. He nodded at Happy with what Peter assumed was the closest thing the Russian had to a polite smile.

"Sorry about cutting to the chase," he glanced briefly at Peter. "Now that I do not work for Mother Russia, my job is harder. Rupert begged for forgiveness; he had a choking deadline to attend. Chen will return to San Francisco with me."

"I will see you across the street, Peter." Happy nodded, "I have a few things to discuss, and I do not want to take away your opportunity to interview my brother. That *is* what you are interested in, Peter?" she teased. Peter mirrored her smile, involuntarily shaking 'no' with his head.

"Nice meeting you, Mr. Marcov."

"And you, Mr. Holland." Turning to Happy, Sergei said, "My dear, we must work out a wrinkle in our plans. Let us talk more with Chen." He put his hand on her shoulder and escorted her to the table.

Happy and Sergei returned to the table nearest the outdoor flagstone fireplace topped with corrugated steel. Peter did not like how easily and tenderly Sergei touched her hand.

Peter opened the patio door, returned to the Twenty-Eight, and found the seating underway for dinner. He found George and Aunt Em at a private table slightly separated from the dining area,

Happy walked into the restaurant minutes later, her red leather skirt accentuated her figure in motion. *'Now, this is one lady I could fall hard for.'* Peter thought.

Happy made straight for her chair next to Aunt Em and Peter.

She kissed her aunt, "You look wonderful, Em. How is the hip feeling?"

"Oh, just marvelous, dear," Aunt Em replied. "Is this your new beau?" she motioned toward Peter.

Happy laughed, "Aunt Em, you are wicked! Peter is here to interview George. And besides, he does not even have my telephone number." She winked at him, teasing both him and Em.

"George, I understand you're staying in town tonight?" she asked her brother.

"Yes. The Governor wants a personal preview of the software. How can I say no to Governor Davis? Besides, it is not bad for business or press coverage." George raised an eyebrow at his sister. "Not to mention several large contracts with the State. I hope you do not mind taking Peter back to his car in Berkeley?" he asked.

"I will be happy to drive Mr. Holland to his car. He may want to interview me," Happy said in a not-so-subtle tease.

"How is your deal working out, Happy?" asked George. "Peter well may want to develop a story on you after your risk partners sign the financing package."

"George, I can't talk about it right now." Happy protested, not too convincingly. "It is supposed to be all hush-hush. I cannot have charming reporters around knowing my business."

Peter had been watching the siblings' interaction with an easy smile. Being around Happy was an accelerant high. "Happy. I am not always a reporter, you know."

"Well, that's a relief, Peter," said Happy. Their gazes met, and Peter felt an inexplicable attraction pull his attention.

After a great dinner, the evening was winding down. The fare consisted of seven courses. Complementing the dishes were five wines, including the aperitif. The wine steward used his wrist to pour on the last glass at the table and left the table.

"I liked the blackened salmon; using the caramelized apricots was a very nice touch," George commented.

Happy hummed, "If you ask me, George, I thought the Merlot was heavenly." She glanced at her aunt, taking in her distant and drooping gazes. "I think Em is getting tired."

George glanced at Em, nodding, "I hope you two don't mind me taking her home now?"

George reached for the bill, briefly glancing over the charges.

"Early a.m. for me." George sighed as he rose from his chair.

George helped Em up, "Sweetie, take good care of your young man. It was so good to see you, Happy," sparkled Aunt Em. There was a mischievous smile on her face.

"You are naughty, Em!" Happy laughed, getting up to hug her aunt goodbye, "It was so good to see you up and about."

After George and Aunt Em had left, Happy rose from her seat, and Peter followed suit. As they exited the restaurant, Happy gave the valet ticket to the attendant, and she asked, "Still need that ride back to the Bay Area, Pete?" She paused. "Is it all right if I call you Pete, isn't it?"

"You can call me anything," Peter responded. "My friends call me Pete. I am not sure if you consider a reporter as a friend?" Peter said teasingly. He spotted the flirting smile across her lips as the valet pulled up in her red BMW convertible with its top up. The valet got out and handed Happy the keys, holding her door open. She unlocked Peter's door, and he got in the car.

"If you would be so kind, it shouldn't be too far out of the way."

"Only if it helps with positive press, Pete." Happy answered his last jab. "Who is Jean?"

"An ex-girlfriend." Peter's reply was curt.

"Sounds not so ex?"

"She left me for greener pastures and found weeds growing. I am very over her." Peter answered, shrugging.

"Good to know!" Happy beamed.

She pulled into the 'N' Street traffic, deftly upshifting, catching both lights at 28th and 29th, and banked hard onto the Capitol Expressway ramp. After a few breathtaking maneuvers and two mergers of traffic, the late model BMW convertible was in the fast lane of Highway 50, heading toward the Bay Area.

**Carquinez Straits**

The massive Carquinez Straits Bridge was like an eight-hundred-pound gorilla to the City of Crocket. The exit was right off the bridge.

Mike stayed back, following the Mercedes off the freeway as the roadway wound underneath the massive piers of twin steel cantilevered bridges. The S600 turned left towards downtown Crocket. The driver parked near a payphone.

Mike killed his car lights and rolled to a stop behind a trash-hauling pickup truck. The hauling company had driven the rusty wreck to its end. The salt air had rotted away its aqua-blue paint. A load of cardboard from broken-down boxes sagged within the peeling plywood sides of the truck bed. Four posts from the body supported the steel rack that held salvaged 4 x 8 plywood sheets and a handful of two by fours. Mike watched through his windshield as the driver crossed the street to make a call on the payphone. After a short conversation, he got back into the car and pulled a U-turn, passing Mike, who leaned over the gearshift, laying low to remain unseen.

**Happy's BMW**

After a few miles, as the beamer started crossing the Yolo Bypass, the moon reflected off the miles of water that plied its way through the artificially controlled floodplain protecting the Capitol. The rain has been unrelenting lately.

The extensive flood plain protects Sacramento and much of Sacramento Valley. Directly above the City, the Sacramento Weir diverts the river by lowering several of the weir's forty-eight gates. In intense flows, the Sacramento River will reverse course for miles taking the excess of the American River's flow away from the Metro Area.

The gates were half open and had been so for the past ten days of rain. The rain gods were smiling upon California, a semi-arid western region. Sacramento has a history of significant floods.

It had the highest risk of flooding in any large metropolitan area, including New Orleans. It also had its share of luck, as in 1986. The city was five hours from being evacuated when the jet stream pushed the pineapple express south to Fresno for a crucial thirty-six hours. The rain returned and continued for several days. Fortunately, the crest of the flood had time to pass Sacramento. The largest dams got relief and continued their release.

Happy settled behind the wheel.

"I parked in the BART Ashby lot," Peter said in a winsome way. He waited for a beat. "I didn't get a chance to compliment you on how great you look tonight, Happy."

Happy smirked. "I bet you say that to all the girls, Pete."

"You're the first one tonight," Peter teased back with a broad smile.

There was another pause before he asked, "Why Happy?"

Happy gave him a quizzical look before returning her gaze to the open road.

"Happy? I mean, your name is...unusual."

"My parents have a twisted sense of humor," she shrugged nonchalantly. "And it runs in the family if you had not noticed with Aunt Em, Pete. They were camping at Caples Lake, planning a day hike along the waist of Carson Pass above Kirkwood. In the afternoon, when they arrived, they set up camp and followed the sound of the creek fed by the lake. Alongside the creek, they made me."

Peter studied Happy as she casually told the tale of her conception.

"My dad's sperm met my mother's egg on the hiking trail the next day. They were lucky not to get electrocuted by the afternoon lightning storm. The State began to burn that day, with five thousand lightning strikes in an outbreak along six-hundred miles of the Sierra. Anyway, I was born, and they were happy campers, and that is where the name came from," she concluded.

"So, you're naturally electric then?" Peter asked, unabashedly flirting with her.

"I am glad you noticed," she cast a sideways glance his way. "What about you, Mr. Holland?"

"Pete, please," Peter said. "I grew up in Chicago; movies in the Loop, Science, and Industry Museum got me into technology in first grade."

Just then, Peter's phone rang. He paused, shooting Happy an apologetic look before answering.

"Peter, I am meeting someone tomorrow. You and Happy, you should meet. Boulevard at eight if you can make it. Ask Happy if she would like to come as well." George's voice crackled through the speakerphone.

Peter lowered the phone from his ear. "George wants us over for dinner tomorrow. Are you free? Want to say hello?"

Happy leaned sideways, and Peter held his phone out, "Hi George, it was great seeing Em. Yes, I am free." Peter's nostrils flared as he took in the scent of her perfume. "But not easy, Pete."

Peter laughed. After the call, he talked about his upbringing in Chicago, the summers in Wisconsin as a youth, driving along Lakeshore Drive as a teenager, and going downtown for movies in the Loop. He liked the Science and Industry Museum as a kid growing up, creating a thirst for knowledge.

Before he knew it, Happy was taking the Ashby off-ramp. She pulled the car into the BART lot next to Peter's older model Q45. Peter felt his heart sink at the realization that the drive was over. He would see her at eight tomorrow regardless, he told himself. But it had been nice to drive over together and be surrounded by her laughter, constant teasing, and flirting.

"Peter, I had fun; we really should do this again," Happy said, smiling softly. Peter exited the car and turned around, his hands resting on her car hood as he leaned down a little.

"Thanks for the ride, Happy. I enjoyed the trip back. George has my number if you need it" he hinted.

"I will wait until you start your car," she gestured toward his car. "Good luck with your story. George likes you," she called out as he walked away. Happy rolled up her window as he returned to his car. After belting himself in, Peter put the keys into the ignition, and the Q started promptly; he turned on his lights and waved to Happy.

She put her car in gear and, with a wave, drove off. Peter reached into his jacket pocket and pulled out his notepad and tape recorder, placing them on the passenger seat. As he merged onto the main road, he realized he needed to talk to Harry about the day and how things had turned out. Harry would be happy about the Camper interview. They would have to plan the cover of the next issue of *Upside*. Then where to meet to drive to Intel the next day.

He glanced at the passenger seat again and saw only the tape recorder and notepad. Peter patted his coat pockets with one hand, hoping to feel the familiar shape of his phone in one of them.

He closed his eyes briefly, cursing himself as he realized he had left his phone in Happy's car.

# Skates

Peter had been so distracted by how much he enjoyed Happy's presence he had left his phone on her dashboard. *What an idiot*, he thought, turning the wheel, then racing out of the parking lot. He turned left onto Ashby Avenue. Ashby ran through a part of the city with a mix of low-rise buildings and scruffy homes on either side. He set his sights on her red BMW, almost catching up to her at San Pablo Avenue at the old Heinz Cannery.

He passed Ashby Lumber, confident that Happy would return to the city. Peter spotted her beamer going over the Highway 80 overpass and stepped on the gas, accelerating to catch up. Happy's BMW turned right onto the access road along the Bay's mud flats and dashed east. Peter worked to keep up. The frontage road was less congested than Highway 80.

Her car turned onto the Berkeley Marina, and Peter followed Happy's car along its South shore to the Skates Restaurant. Peter parked just in time to catch her walking across the gangway to the waterfront restaurant on San Francisco Bay. He got out, dashing to follow her.

The restaurant thrust out into the bay upon pilings into the approaching fog. He walked into the stilted establishment by a boardwalk built over the twenty-foot-deep mudflat and water. Skates' glass walls frame the San Francisco Bay, the Bay Bridge, and the city. Peter looked around, checking for Happy. He walked through the bar, scanning for her familiar face.

Realizing she might be in the ladies' room, Peter decided to go to the men's room. He stood in front of the mirror, washing his hands as he appraised himself in the mirror.

"You're not twenty-five anymore, but you're all I got," he muttered, running a hand through his hair to look effortless and presentable.

Peter opened the door in time to see Happy finishing a call on her cell phone.

"Yes, I will wait another five minutes. See you then." She hung up the phone, turning around. Happy spotted Peter instantly, and her brows arched in surprise and amusement.

Peter realized how this must have seemed. He did follow her back, but he had a genuine reason to. He looked relieved, unable to mask his embarrassment and affection.

"I couldn't stay away," he said, sheepishly adding, "I left my phone in your car."

Happy grinned, flashing her beautiful, straight teeth. "You sure have that phone pickup line down, don't you, Pete?"

Peter was unable to help the smile on his face and enjoyed the sound of his nickname on her lips.

"Seems like you needed a drink after dropping me off," he commented. Peter wanted to sound sly but wondered if it came off as self-deprecating.

"No, Pete, I had one last meeting tonight. A couple of signatures were missing on an offer." She turned around. "Let's get your phone."

As they exited the restaurant, Sergei Marcov entered the establishment. The Russian's steps faltered slightly, surprise unmistakable on his face. He had not expected Peter to be here.

"Hi, Sergei," Happy waved nonchalantly. "I need to rescue a phone for Pete. I will be right back."

Sergei bowed. "Mr. Holland."

He held the door open for them as they stepped out. Peter could feel the Russian's malevolent glare burning into the back of his skull.

He noticed an SUV pulling up next to Sergei's imposing Mercedes. They reached Happy's car, and she retrieved his phone. Peter felt her caressing his hand as she handed him the phone.

"Peter, you don't need the phone as an excuse anymore," she teased. "Here's my card."

"Thanks." His hands were closed around the phone. "I needed to call my editor about today's interview with your brother. I do not want to keep you."

Happy smiled, stepping closer to him. She leaned into him, making Peter's breath catch as they hugged. Happy touched his jaw, angling his face for a soft, lingering kiss. She pulled away a hand on his neck as she brought his ear to her lips. "You can keep me, Pete," she whispered.

Peter could feel his heartbeat drumming in his ears. Masking his surprise, his hands circled her waist as he returned the kiss. His lips brushed against her softly before he deepened the kiss.

"I said you're electric," he began, his voice low. "But I may need to lower your wattage."

Happy smiled against his lips. "I don't want to burn you, Pete."

She finished the sentence with another kiss. Her eyes fluttered closed, the kiss tender and bottomless. It ended as quickly as it had begun. Peter opened his eyes in time to catch her grinning as she strutted away from him across the street into the restaurant. Peter watched her. His expression was wistful as she swung her hips into the approaching fog.

His thoughts veered away from Happy as an Asian man approached the limo and got in. Peter recognized him as Lee, the man he had met in Sacramento. The chauffeur door opened moments later, and a massive, meaty driver with a buzz cut appeared. He glanced around furtively before opening the rear door. Lin and Kai Lee appeared and got in the sport utility vehicle. The SUV driver got out and into the limo driver's seat.

Happy entered the restaurant and found Sergei waiting for her near the host station.

"We need a quiet table," Sergei said to the hostess.

"Follow me." She spoke and led them to a table facing the bay, separated from the other diners.

"I do not want this Mr. Holland knowing our business, Happy. The young man is interested in you, yes? We do not want the press to question the export license we were just awarded." Sergei said.

"Peter is interviewing my brother about his security software. And I do not talk out of class." Happy said, her tone pointed.

"I am sorry to caution you. We are close to concluding the business side of our relationship. I hoped to discuss travel later to unwind from all our work." Sergei's eyebrow raised.

"Sergei, I never mix work with pleasure, and I am not about to start breaking my rules." Happy opened her satchel and pulled out a contract. "Sign on pages three and page ten."

"Ok, OK, I will let it rest for now. Here is the contract. We should license your brother's software for the project, yes?" Sergei asked as he handed the contract back to Happy. He caressed her hand briefly as she took the contract from him.

"I will bring it up with George tomorrow at dinner." Happy said as she stood up to leave.

## Peter's Car

Peter shook his head, getting into his car. He dialed Harry, his gaze still on the two vehicles, Happy's BMW, and the black Mercedes of Sergei's Something about the setup unsettled him.

"Harry, it is Peter. I spent the day with George Camper at the Capitol and had a long interview."

"Great to hear, Pete," Harry's voice crackled through the speaker. "When am I going to see the story?"

"I think I'm on to something, big," Peter responded. "I rode back to the Bay Area with Camper's sister. She is a venture capital up-

and-comer. Let us meet in Emeryville and drive to Intel in the morning."

The call ended, and a soft song on the radio reminded Peter of the intimate moments he had shared with Happy moments ago. His gaze was set on the restaurant front, but his thoughts were distant. He returned to reality as Happy and Sergei appeared from the restaurant, deep in conversation.

Peter watched how Sergei looked at her. A comment from him made her laugh. He could tell the Russian was flirting with her. Happy went in for a quick hug before leaving Sergei on the sidewalk, crossing to her car, then driving off.

Peter's gaze narrowed, his face betraying his distrust of Sergei. "What are you up to?" he whispered to himself.

Sergei looked around before walking toward the waiting SUV. Sergei shouted in Russian to the SUV's driver, then got into the Mercedes. Moments later, both vehicles pulled away from the curb.

Peter put his car in gear, following them. He stayed a reasonable distance behind them, following the Mercedes out of the Marina and onto Highway 80, west toward San Francisco. As the night air cooled, the fog descended, enveloping the bridge in a blanket of gray.

The SUV and limo exited Ninth Street, crossing over Van Ness on Hayes, and turning right on Franklin Street. They crossed Gary and traveled downhill to Broadway; the limo turned left while the SUV went straight ahead.

Peter turned left on Broadway following Sergei in the Mercedes. The conditions did not make it easy; visibility had become dangerous on the steep hill road. The street looked as if it had ended in a cloud. Similarly, the expensive, well-maintained mansions lining at the end of Broadway had become hard to see.

## Broadway and Baker Street

A stately Italian Renaissance style mansion appeared through the fog at Baker Street as if it were a rampart to repel the mist. The Mercedes stopped on the downhill side curb, and the fog gave them all the cover they might need. Inside, Sergei mulled things over. He tapped his ring against his cocktail glass. He took a sip, his severe expression changing to an empty, reassuring smile as he turned to Rupert Lee.

Lee met his gaze hesitantly. The nervous tremor in his leg gave away his desire to reunite with his family. He just wanted to be finished with this maniacal Russian.

"Lee," Sergei began, his accent thick. "Your family is down the steps on the street below. The driver will take you and your family to the new life I have arranged for you."

Lee was wary, waiting for his following words.

"I need your final design and encryption code. Now." Sergei finished.

The lines on Lee's brow smoothed out as he handed Sergei the disc. "Here is the final design. I am glad to be done with it." As Sergei reached out to grasp the disc, Lee held on. Sergei arched a brow at him in question.

"You already have the encryption codes. They are on the first dis. Be careful not to lose it," Lee warned. "The 256-bit encryption is randomly generated. I have no means to recover it."

Sergei smiled, though, to Lee, it seemed like a sinister sneer. The scar on his face deepened as he dismissed Lee. "Thank you, Lee, here are the green cards for your family," he said. "May you and your family never be separated again!"

Lee opened the door and stepped out. He stood on the curb as the Mercedes drove away. He looked around nervously before descending the staircase.

**Peter's Car**

Peter's car was halfway down the block on Broadway, hidden by the thick fog. The street was wet. Tree branches dripped onto the leaves that covered the sidewalk. The reporter saw a man appear from the limo and stand there while the limo drove away into the mist. A foghorn echoed through the borough. Peter exited his car, closing the car door behind him.

The door clunked loudly on the seatbelt buckle, blocking the latch. The sound echoed off the brick retaining wall and to the man up the street. He turned to the noise.

"FUCK!" Peter whispered to himself.

The man quickly disappeared down a set of steps. Peter quietly made his way up the street and to the staircase. He heard nothing but dead calm. The moan of the foghorn sounded again. There was no other sound save for the occasional water dripping onto the sidewalk. At the top of the steps, a black cat scurried into the bushes. Peter descended the staircase.

Unaware of the silent reporter in pursuit and finally free of Sergei, Lee eagerly bounded down the steps. He passed a dark entryway, and after he passed, driver Boris emerged from the shadows to follow him.

He grabbed Lee from behind. A thick wire wrapped around Lee's throat as Boris garroted him on the landing. Lee's eyes opened wide with panic, he struggled desperately against the wire, choking, gagging, as spittle flew from his mouth.

Peter continued down the staircase warily, hesitating as Lee's guttural, choking sounded in his ears. He felt his skin crawl. Before he could respond, a large, heavy-set man was making his way up the steps, grunting with effort. Peter scrambled to hide in the dark entryway just as car tires squealed to a stop on the street above. A car door opened and closed, and a voice from the roadway above shouted, "Stay right where you are!"

The big man retreated down the steps at the command, heavy footfalls vanishing in the fog. The car above raced away while a car door below the steps slammed closed. Peter's breathing was harsh. He struggled to calm down. He turned, ascending the steps to find only an empty, foggy road. The foghorn sounded once more.

**Sergei's Limo**

Sergei sipped his drink, holding the disk in his other hand, satisfied. His phone rang. Sergei put the glass down then answered the call.

"Da?"

"Boss, I had to leave Lee on the steps," Boris said, his voice breathy.

Sergei sat forward, his expression changing instantly, face red with rage. "What do you say, Boris?" he roared.

"Someone was coming down the stairs as I finished him," Boris answered. "With the FBI surveillance around the Consulate, I thought it better to care for my cargo."

Sergei sighed, looking upwards, searching for the perfect answer. His mood changed suddenly, the rage disappearing as he lightly said, "That was wise, Boris. When do you go fishing?"

"As soon as the fog thins, Boss."

Sergei ended the call. He was about to set his mobile aside when it rang again.

**General Chen's Hotel Room**

The computer screen outlined in blue the weathered face and piercing eyes of General Chen. His brow furrowed in unease and frustration as he stubbed out his cigarette, pressing auto-dial on his speakerphone.

"Comrade, is Lee still with us?"

There was a beat of silence. "No, why do you ask?"

"The disk you delivered is not the chip design. Are you changing our arrangement?" Chen crushed out his cigarette, showing his displeasure and frustration.

Sergei cleared his throat. "I do not know what you are talking about, Chen. I gave my driver Boris the disk to deliver directly to your consulate after our video call."

Chen inhaled deeply. "I have only a business plan for a video conference network."

Moments passed in silence as Sergei's dismay turned to frustration. His scar deepened with fury on his face.

"Chen, I will take care of it immediately. I know what happened exactly." Sergei practically growled as he ended one call and placed another. "When you are back from fishing, Boris, be ready for another trip."

### Rodriguez Conan 65 – San Francisco Yacht Club

The San Francisco Yacht Club was eerily silent pre-dawn. Boris approached the berth of a large sports fishing boat, a 65-footer with a white, gel-coated hull. The boat's twin radar domes topping the flying bridge made an impressive profile. Boris waited for dawn in a fog growing denser by the minute.

He held a phone to his ear, listening to Sergei, and watching the crew drag the body bags of Lee's brother and sister onto the boat deck. As a foghorn sounded through the harbor, Boris answered his boss.

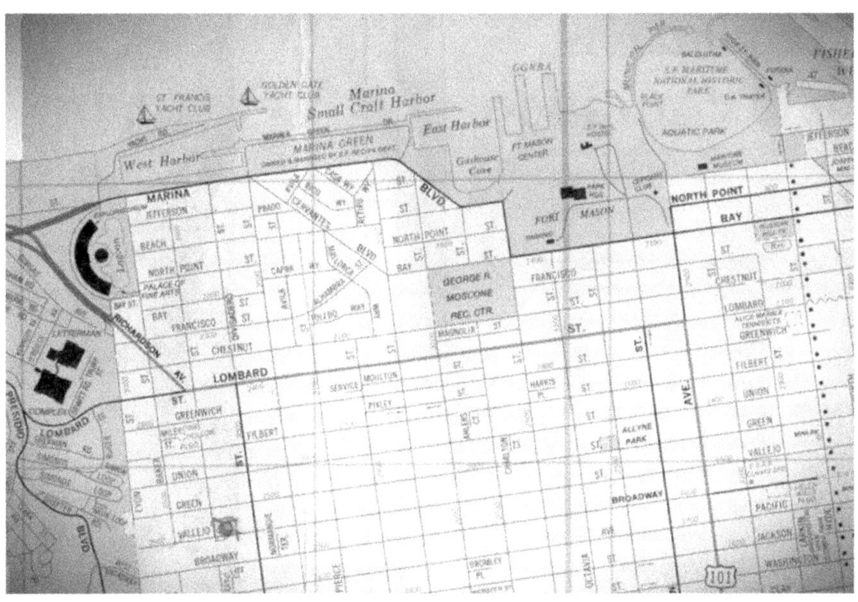

"Da, da, da, I have it, Boss, as soon as I finish...fishing. First thing I get back, promise." Boris yelled up to Dimitri, "Cast off." Dimitri started the twin engines while Boris freed the bow lines. The crewmen looped the tie lines off the dock. Dimitri at the helm, reversed the starboard engine and gently eased out of the slip. A foghorn moaned as he loaded its top-of-the-line navigation system on the control screen.

# Day Three - Emergency Room

## Jorge Esparante's Villa, Guadalajara

A light breeze rustled the curtains of the expensive open windows of the French revival-style living room. Jorge wore a white linen jacket over a Tommy Bahamas silk shirt, beige silk slacks, and hand-tooled loafers.

Esparante, a short, thin man in his sixties held a large cigar loosely between two fingers. Looking out the windows over his sprawling estate, he exhaled, his gaze following the cigar smoke as it curled past his shoulder out the window.

A trim, handsome, dark-haired young man in white slacks and a black silk shirt approached, Jorge's trusted lieutenant, Enrico. He carried a tray with a bottle of scotch, a clean crystal glass, and ice in a silver container.

"Our first shipment to our Russian friend was uneventful; the diamond quality paid is exceptional," Enrico said, his accent revealing his Venezuelan origins.

Jorge nodded in satisfaction, "Thank you, Enrico. I will have no further need for you tonight," he said in heavily accented English. "Take your senorita out. You have earned it."

Enrico bent to pour scotch into Jorge's crystal glass and took his leave with a slight bow. Jorge dropped an ice cube into his drink, pondering over the news. He glanced at the time on his Rolex Submariner and picked up his cell phone from the ornate console table. He lifted the glass to his lips. With his cigar held firmly between his fingers, he dialed a number with his other hand and waited serenely for the connection.

"Sergei, I'm pleased with our first business."

"I'm also pleased with our transaction," the Russian replied from the other end. "How can I help?"

Jorge's expression darkened, "My friends tell me you can help us with our information problem. I have unfinished business I need to...eliminate."

**Peter's Bedroom**

Peter Holland was roused from sleep at 3:30 in the morning by a scratchy feeling in his throat. He swung his legs to the floor. Still groggy, he got up to gargle, crossing the dark bedroom. He stepped over the floor heater and caught his foot on something jutting out.

"Fuck!" he yelled as he jammed his foot into the floor heater's vent key.

"That hurt." He hopped around the apartment for a few minutes, using his entire vocabulary of four-letter words, afraid he broke his toe. The loft's white walls reached up to well-placed skylights. Modern art hung from every wall in the two-story apartment. IKEA bookshelves filled the space in between the windows and Peter had chosen low-slung coffee tables and couches in caramel-colored wood and teal-colored leather cushions for the living space.

Peter tentatively tried bearing weight on his damaged toe. He thought he would live. Relief was his first thought. Nothing seemed broken. However, his sock was soaking wet.

After making his way to the bathroom, Peter relieved himself. The pain in his foot had subsided, but the underside of his foot still felt wet. He lifted it briefly, cursing under his breath as he saw the small pool of blood on the bathroom floor.

Peter sat on the toilet and pulled off his socks to look. He looked down, watching a puddle of blood grow around his toes. Instinctively stepping over the heater grate, he launched the key's end into the web of his toes.

His exploring fingers could only feel an unending hole between his small and next toe on his left foot. Realizing this was not a situation for a Band-Aid, he stuffed toilet paper into the wound and wrapped his foot in a hand towel.

He searched for something to tape in place. He balanced on one foot as he pulled out the ace bandage from his medicine cabinet, growling as he did a half-assed job at bandaging his foot.

"I am going to need more than Hydrogen Peroxide and a bandage," he sighed.

*'The Kaiser ER is the best bet,'* he thought.

"It shouldn't be too crowded this time of the week," he said as he hobbled out of the house and to his car. He drove up 45th Street toward San Pablo, turned right, and headed to Oakland.

**Rodriguez Conan 65 Golden Gate**

With the high tide's current at six knots coming in, Dimitri pilots the boat, hugging the shoreline with the eddy current, under the Golden Gate Bridge. Dense fog wrapped around the city, hiding the top of the massive South Tower approach sheltering the Fort Point Civil War Fortress. A foghorn sounded through the eerie mist as ten Mississippi rivers of ingressive water flowed to the right.

**Emergency Room**

The last time he needed Kaiser's emergency room, he had been helping his sister at her Berkeley art gallery opening, keeping an eye on her precocious niece. Good thing for his sister, six-year-old Juleah had plenty of kids to play with within the old soup kitchens of the Heinz Factory at San Pablo and Ashby in Berkeley.

The kids were running around, needing only the occasional corralling. Suddenly a shrieking sound came from the office. Juleah had been knocked onto a couch and landed on an intern's backpack. The backpack had an artist's knife unsheathed inside. The extremely sharp and long blade had first scraped her bottom, and when she turned over, the blade penetrated her knee.

Using a clean towel for a compress, Peter came to the rescue and asked for directions to the hospital. His sister was expecting a wealthy buyer for the new show, so Peter insisted on taking Juleah to the emergency room for repairs.

It was a madhouse in the hospital. Fortunately, the staff took Juleah sooner than later, promptly taking care of her injuries. Now, it was Peter's turn to visit the same emergency room.

The traffic was light; there was even a parking spot on the same side of the street. Peter hobbled into the emergency room. Thankfully, there was no line at Reception.

"Your name, please," a nurse asked as he approached.

"Peter Holland."

"Hi, Peter. What is troubling you?"

"I just put a hole in my foot, and it was gushing blood before I wrapped it and drove over here; I don't know if it has stopped."

"Stay right there," she said, pressing a button on her handset. "Gurney to the waiting room."

A large, pleasant, black orderly, his dreadlocks tied behind his neck, rolled a gurney through the double doors.

"Get on, Mr. Holland, you are going to Exam Three and Dr. Chinn. He is expecting you." the nurse said.

The orderly told Peter to "Climb aboard," in a heavily Jamaican-accented voice. "You have no worries with me, man."

The gurney pushed through the automatic doors, the orderly whisking Peter down the ER hallway leading to Exam Room Three.

**Golden Gate**

The waves were choppy now, as the Japanese current going south fought the tide coming in. The Pacific had been calm for the past week, slacking between storms.

The swells were large enough that the waves crashed over the fishing boat's bow fighting its way against the swell out into the Bay. Armored with heavy-duty brass portholes battened for rough seas, the ship was fitted for ocean travel. The radar was in order, as was their course. The vessel passed the red navigation lights on the south pier fender while the south tower foghorn sounded.

**Kaiser Emergency Room**

Peter's luck started to change as they rolled him through the doors; a siren preceded the arrival of a trauma case.

Looking up only briefly to see if she was needed, a young black nurse returned to performing a rapid triage on Peter. He noticed her name, Jenny, on her brass name badge.

"Mr. Holland, good job on the dressing," Jenny said. "It looks like you stopped the bleeding."

She glanced at the wound, "The injury looks deep. I am sure the doc will want an X-ray of your foot before he does anything."

"Thanks, Jenny. I am glad to have you look at it," said Peter to no one in particular. "What's the crime tape all about on that hallway?"

The nurse grimaced, pain flitting across her features momentarily before it was replaced by deadpan professionalism, "This morning, Dr. Morse was hammered to death by a person with a mental health condition. He was a brilliant trauma surgeon, a real shame he is gone."  A commotion out in the hall made the nurse turn around, "I will look in on you in a few moments; there is a gunshot victim rolling in. I will be right back," Nurse Peters said as she rushed away.

The next couple of hours passed like a week for Peter. A druggie OD'd, and the staff worked hard to rouse an older street person who had collapsed on a sidewalk nearby. He was finally conscious, and they had to redouble their efforts to keep him awake.

Eventually, they forced the guy to drink something that made him puke up his stomach contents, mostly over himself and the ER interns.

The staff uttered many choice words as an unpleasant smell wafted into the hallway. Peter nodded off to sleep, his throbbing foot marking the passage of time.

**Farallon Islands**

Pre-dawn in the water saw two crewmen tossing buckets of chum bait over the side of the fishing boat near the Farallon Islands.

## Kaiser Emergency Room

Walking up, Marley, the black orderly, said, "Hey, mon, what are you doing here, all by your lonesome?"

"I thought I would guard the crime scene," Peter responded slowly, "You know I am an undercover cop? I have my eye on you. I heard about Dr. Morris."

"Some crazy man has been killing doctors around the East Bay." A sad expression overcame his usually beaming face.

"I don't know if I feel better knowing that after laying here for a couple of hours alone," he muttered.

The big man shook his head, smiling, "Mon, I have to take you down to the big machine now." He wheeled him away, stopping the gurney and pushing the down button of the elevator door with his elbow.

"Make sure they give you an extra lead skirt." The elevator doors opened, and he rolled Peter out, "You don't want no two-headed kids, right?"

The doors at the opposite end opened onto the basement corridor. Peter took in the room as Marley wheeled him into X-ray; in the corner stood a control panel wedged behind a thick, shielded wall; the table looked like something out of the Fantastic Four's laboratory, and the machine's large emitter head reminded him of a praying mantis.

Juleah had been great to this point, Peter recalled. He had kept her engaged, pointing out details of the room to her, anything to keep her mind off what was coming next, shots, needles, and pain.

Peter always liked to make a game of going anywhere with his favorite niece. How much could he explain to a growing young mind and not bore her? Juleah's technician, a handsome young internist, was great and explained everything.

"Mr. Holland, can you lift your foot for a moment?" said the female technician.

"Please hold this position until I tell you to relax," she adjusted the lead blanket over the more vulnerable parts of Peter's anatomy. The technician turned and walked behind the corner pony wall, double-checking the settings and alignments.

Peter heard a deeper sound than that of the dentist's office X-ray. It sounded like a bug zapper on steroids, of sci-fi machines battling giant ants in the distance.

"Okay, Mr. Holland, I need you to lay on your side—we will do a full rotation of your foot."

Peter shifted.

"They are unsure if you will need surgery," the technician said, sounding unnaturally perky. "The wound came extremely near to your bone. We need to see if it is damaged."

He nodded, realizing that the technician could not see him anyway.

"If it is, we have an OR ready for you."

"An operation?" he piped up.

"When a wound penetrates so deeply and chips the bone, we must take infection very seriously, Mr. Holland," she answered.

They wheeled Peter back to the elevator after being turned like a rotisserie chicken at a Banderas restaurant.

**Farallon Islands**

The yacht slowed to an idle, and Dimitri trimmed the thrusters to keep the bow in the waves. He enabled the aft controls and turned on the floodlights on the fantail. He climbed downstairs and joined the other men below. They wrestled the body bags onto the fantail.

### Kaiser Emergency Room

Peter clasped his hands above his stomach as he lay on a gurney in a dimly lit green corridor outside the X-ray room. The police crime scene tape still blocked the passage to a hallway nearby. A plump older nurse with grey hair in green scrubs approached him, nodding as she wheeled him toward the examination room.

"We are going to miss Dr. Morris."

*'Better him and not me,'* thought Peter.

The nurse steered him into the exam room, replacing her dark demeanor with a much pluckier attitude, "Don't make it a habit coming in here, okay? You do not know what you can catch."

Peter was shifted to the examination table as a maintenance worker cleared another exam table of bloodied sponges from what Peter learned was a gang shooting trauma case. A stressed young ER resident with glasses and a two-day beard shrugged on a clean white coat over his bloodied scrubs, sighing as he adjusted his glasses.

He bent over Peter's wound and started rinsing it, "You were lucky," he announced. "The heater key punctured an inch-deep hole in your toe webbing but missed the bone. You would be in surgery if it broke your bone."

He adjusted a light into position, "I'm thoroughly irrigating the wound to prevent infection," he said before snapping on a clean pair of surgical gloves. He dried off Peter's foot then injected with a local anesthetic before suturing the wound. "This should not hurt. Sorry, it took so long to get to you, we had several gunshot cases, and the ER is still coming to grips since Dr. Morse's death today."

Peter tried not to look at the procedure, "It was a little unnerving to be in that hallway by myself. It sounds like they caught the guy."

The doctor hummed in thought, pausing momentarily before dressing the wound. As another trauma case wheeled into the ER, the doctor glanced up before meeting Peter's gaze.

**Farallon Islands**

As the sun broke the horizon, The body bags lay empty on the deck of the yacht. Dimitri swung the boat around for one final look. Boris and Igor were hosing down the boat, washing off the bits and pieces of their work.

**Kaiser Emergency Room**

It was eight in the morning before Peter got out of the ER.

"I want you to elevate your foot for the next several days as much as you can," the doctor said, sights already set on the following case. "Come back in ten days to have the stitches taken out. Got to go!"

"Thanks, doc," Peter said, primarily to himself, as the resident rushed away. The sound of a siren grew louder outside.

**Marcov's Mercedes Limousine**

Sergei's phone rang.

"What do you mean it is not there? I told you to check his office," Sergei stared at the moon roof. "You did. He is out. Well, then find him. I repeat we must get that disc."

**Broadway and Baker**

The fog infiltrated the crime scene. Several police cars, reporters, and a coroner's van stood at the top of the Baker steps. Mike's SUV pulled up near the intersection. The sight of the reporters aggravated him. The last thing they needed was the media on the case. He got out of the car and walked to the officer in charge. Lieutenant

Joe Brick was a medium-height, dark-haired man in his fifties. He had a wrestler's build that his gray raincoat could not conceal.

Four men ascended the last steps to the street with a gurney and dropped its wheels on the roadway, promptly rolling it toward the coroner's van. Mike waved his ID as he walked over to the gurney, motioning to the coroner to open the body bag, revealing Lee's face.

"Do you have an ID on him?"

Joe Brick sneezed, working through his severe head cold, a cold that obscured his usual midwestern accent.

"He was Rupert Lee; he had an Intel security badge and a Folsom address," he said sourly. "It looks like he is a technical guy. Garroted, and then his throat slashed, not a pleasant way to go, but quick. I have seen this once in Chinatown, but not Pacific Heights." His grimace told Mike he was in a bad mood.

Mike passed his card to Lieutenant Brick and leaned closer. "Lieutenant, my card; call me when you have anything," he said emphatically. "I'm very interested in this case."

Brick glanced at his card before pocketing it, "I did mean to ask you why the FBI is here, but knowing the Russian Consulate is a block away…."

Mike raised an eyebrow firmly, not taking the bait, "Don't ask; call me with anything. Okay?"

"A storm is coming in. Do not bother cleaning the steps." Brick told his team, "The rain will wash away the blood."

**Peter's Bedroom**

The sun flooded the loft. Its rays painted the white walls gold, brightening up the entire apartment. Peter's workout clothes lay folded on a chair next to the bed. Bloody footprints painted the floor as Peter Holland lay in bed, his foot propped up on a pillow.

His phone rang, and Peter shifted to reach over to his side table, "Holland here," he answered, coughing slightly. He cleared his throat to get rid of the rasp in his voice. "Harry, can you pick me up at the Holiday Inn in Emeryville? We need to get up to Intel early for the press briefing."

Harry's voice crackled out from the speaker, "Of course. You are on my way."

Peter glanced at his wristwatch, "You drive. I hurt my foot last night." He nodded, rubbing his eyes. "Great, see you in forty."

**Marcov's Mercedes**

Sergei Marcov's car coasted towards the red brick building on tree-lined Green Street as he headed toward the Russian Consulate. The front entrance of the six-story, red-brick Consulate was just past a white iron fence. The red entry door was open. Sergei opened the gate and limped up the three steps that led into the building.

Mike Murphy's phone rang shortly after that.

"Murphy." he told the caller.

"Mike, you won't believe who just walked into the Consulate," Special Agent Jim Joseph spoke from the other end. He stood before a side window of a larger bay window with field glasses mounted on a tripod. "Marcov."

"Jim, thanks for the heads up," he whirled his seat around. "Is the intercept shack still on the roof? In the eighties, the Cow Hollow Association complained about the battleship's gray-painted plywood structure on the top of the consulate, blocking the views of the Golden Gate Bridge."

"Good memory, Mike. They had to use a non-lead-based paint to allow signals to pass to the eavesdropping antennas," Jim had a view of the roof of the Russian Consulate. "When the US 6th Army had its headquarters in the Presidio, the Russians located their consulate in direct line of AT&T's microwave signals from downtown to the Base."

**Russian Consulate**

Sergei entered the brightly lit, white-marbled foyer with ornate wall sconces. The red carpet had golden trim, and Russian flags bookended the reception desk, where a clean-shaven young man in a cheap dark suit straightened his red tie as he noticed Sergei enter the foyer.

He stood at attention. "Comrade Marcov."

"Vulakovich is expecting me."

He nodded, "At once, Comrade."

Vulakovich's office was full of filing cabinets, a few of which had combination locks. His desk was plain and drab, overflowing with reports. A stocky man in a poorly fitted grey suit sat behind the desk before a picture of Vladimir Putin.

"Bring us tea," Vulakovich commanded his aide.

The aide returned with a silver tray, teapot, tea glasses, and sugar. Vulakovich poured Sergei tea and added sugar before lighting a cigarette.

"How can I help a friend of Vladimir, Comrade Marcov?" Vulakovich nodded toward Putin's framed photo.

Sergei tapped his tea glass with his ring after setting it down. He lit a cigar and began, "I have a shortlist for you. Our Chinese friends want to learn how we are hacking the US Military," he fixed Vulakovich with a severe look. "They are interested in Oak Ridge & Los Alamos Labs and promise to share their work. I also need to find John Nord today, who works for the Hyatt conference center."

"Moscow is pleased with your work bringing Russian diamonds to the West," said Vulakovich.

"It is important that the DeBeers Cartel does not restrict Mother Russia's diamond trade. I find them useful in the contraband trade we use to penetrate Silicon Valley's high-tech industry. Sergei responded.

The phone on Vulakovich's desk rang. He answered it after the first ring. He listened briefly, "Comrade, I am sitting with him right now," Vulakovich nodded, "Da, I will pass the phone to him."

Sergei stood up and took the phone. He listened to the person on the other end and nodded several times before returning the phone to Vulakovich.

"We need to find an FBI agent named Mike Murphy for a new partner," Sergei said. "The DEA found out about our recent business, and an old enemy of theirs just surfaced."

Vulakovich nodded in response. There was a knock on the door just then. Before Vulakovich could prompt entry, a black-haired aide with a rugby player's build entered the office. He walked briskly toward Vulakovich's desk and held out the morning paper. He pointed out a story to Vulakovich.

His eyes darted over the text, "The police have recovered a body two blocks away from here. Your work, Sergei?"

"It was necessary but interrupted," Sergei answered curtly.

"I'll have to report this at once."

Sergei winced, rubbing his injured leg with his ring hand, striving to massage the pain, "Of course. You will inform Moscow that the FBI compromised a spy, and a loose end is tied off," Sergei nodded, standing up and pulling his overcoat on. "My leg is telling me a storm is coming."

He limped toward the door and paused briefly, his thoughts going to the aide who had just come in, "Please ask Igor if he is interested in freelance work?"

**Bush Street**

John Nord's faded blue Taurus wagon flowed with the traffic down Bush Street, passing the looming Sutter-Stockton parking garage. Three, four, and seven-story buildings flanked the street. A double-parked delivery truck blocked the right lane near the Grant intersection, where a fire escape landed from a four-story building.

Maxy Roland sang along with a Wham song as he jogged up Grant Street.

*So I'm never gonna dance again*
*The way I danced with…*

John's phone rang as his car neared Grant Avenue. He glanced at his phone for a second, missing the moment when a jogger with headphones over his ears ran through the traffic light without looking in front of John's car.

"No!" he screamed with terror, his eyes squeezing shut as he slammed the brakes, but to no avail.

Moments later, John sat on the steps under the Pagoda Gateway leading into Chinatown. His eyes were burning from tears. He cradled his head as a big-nosed, Irish police officer loomed over him, writing into his leather notebook.

The officer turned and motioned to a Sikh taxi driver in a blue turban with a yellow sleeveless sweater, animatedly talking to another Sikh taxi driver. The Sikh hurried over to the police officer.

"Let's see your license," he said. "Do you know what happened?"

The Sikh taxi driver reached inside his jacket pocket for his license as he told his tale, "No problem. That crazy jogger just ran into traffic without a care in the world," he said. "He ran in front of the station wagon, bounced off, and the bus made him into a chapati."

John looked up at the Sikh in horror as the officer stopped writing and thoughtfully placed his notebook into his back pocket.

"Thanks. I am glad you saw everything," the police officer said awkwardly. "We call it a pancake here. Have a better day."

"Namaste," he said.

The officer said, "You're not at fault; several witnesses have the jogger running in front of your car."

John swallowed thickly, "I just missed him yesterday; the same fucking guy ran before me yesterday. I stood on my brakes, spinning through an intersection, avoiding the guy down the block at Montgomery."

The officer straightened up. "Sorry, you've got to deal with it."

John squeezed his eyes shut as the jogger's horrified face flashed in his memory, the way it had passed by his windshield.

John shook his head, "I could see his face when I hit him," he felt the lump in his throat constrict his breathing as the tears started again. He waved his hands in front of his eyes. "I-I-I can't see."

The officer's brow furrowed at John's distant gaze, "Hey, you, okay?" he waved over the paramedic that had just finished wheeling the gurney with the jogger's body into the ambulance.

"I can't see," John's voice was barely above a whisper.

# The Boulevard

With a cold compress over his eyes, John was twitching on his back on a gurney. A young Asian nurse in a white outfit checked his blood pressure and glanced at his chart. A doctor in his mid-forties escorted Laura to John's station, discussing her fiancé's case with her.

He turned to her, "Has John ever been in combat?"

Laura nodded, worrying at her lip as her thoughts went to his injured leg, "Yes, he was wounded in the leg in Panama."

"That may explain his symptoms. Have you heard of PTSD?"

Laura gave him a thin-lipped smile, "Doctor, I am an RN. What is he presenting?"

"Hysterical blindness," he answered. "I have seen it with a few vets before. The brain disconnects from what it has seen. I need you to see if you can break his connection to the accident."

**San Francisco Yacht Club**

The crew tied the vessel to the dock, and Boris stepped onto the pier, answering his phone as he did so. His fishing trip was over.

"Yes, Boss. Just docked," he said, pausing as he repeated what was said. "Sunset District Ninth and Lawton, John Nord, got it."

Boris lifted his hand in the air, signaling Dimitri over.

"Stay close to your phone and boat. I will need you soon."

**Ninth and Lawton**

John was sitting on the couch downstairs in his wainscoted mission-style home. He held his head in his hands, the accident replaying in his head. Laura tended to him, bending over him in concern, her blonde hair brushing his skin as she embraced him.

"John, you're not at fault," she cooed softly, running her hands through his hair as she cradled his face. "He jogged right in front of you. It is not your fault. I know how you drive. You were not responsible."

John leaned back, breaking away from her embrace, and leaned his head on the back of the couch, a wet towel over his eyes. He grabbed the towel and tossed it across the room.

"Except I killed him," he snapped before leaning back again. "I am cursed. It always comes in threes."

Laura stopped, confused, "It comes in threes? What do you mean?"

John's face drained of all emotion as his gaze became distant. He still could not see, but Laura could tell he was deep in thought.

"I was sixteen, and it was my first week of driving," he recalled. "I drove into the city for a Fillmore show. On the way over to Winters to pick up a friend, I noticed beer cans hurling in the air behind a hedge on a curve. An El Camino comes sliding out of the turn – straight at me with ten kids in the back bed throwing beer cans. We clicked door handles as I drove my Falcon into the shoulder, just missing a telephone pole."

Laura sat beside him, adding hopefully, "It sounds like great defensive driving to me. Not a curse."

John shook his head in refusal. "Then, after picking up my friend in Winters, I checked my mirrors and the road ahead to pass a car. It was clear for miles. I rechecked my mirrors, pulled out to pass, and a motorcycle doing a hundred plus was coming at me. I barely got back into my lane."

Laura nodded, sensing where the story was going.

"That was a close call for the motorcycle."

John's voice lowered as he was transported back to the third incident, "After the show, we were driving back, passing Ashby on eighty. As I overtook a flatbed truck on my right, I saw headlights coming like a bat out of hell in the slow lane. I braked to give him room, but the Corvette hit the end of the steel rebar, overhanging the load. It was a mess."

Laura's brow furrowed with concern, "The first week of driving?"

John's voice was thick as he continued the tale, "Yep. My I-beam miraculous maneuver was after two close calls. What I did not tell you after I cleared the I-beam," he took a shaky breath. "Beyond, there were several car wrecks, and I, I ran over a … little girl lying in the road."

Laura gasped, eyes widening and welling with tears instantaneously as sympathy for John overtook her, "I didn't know how traumatized you have been."

John shuddered, curling in on himself.

"I now know why you're cautious around steel-hauling trucks," she said.

John sighed, "This week, two more close calls, including the jogger. And now he is dead."

Laura bent over him, kissing him several times on his eyes. Tears wet their faces, and a few minutes passed in silence before John could speak.

"I have a consulting job, and possibility of picking up a lease of their video conferencing systems in Scotts Valley tomorrow. Can you drive me down? I do not want to get behind the wheel ever again."

"My car goes into the shop tomorrow. We will have to take your wagon," she paused, hoping John felt lighter. "Are you feeling better?"

"I am—as long as I don't have to drive," John said, his mood far more elevated now than how miserable he felt moments ago.

John's phone rang; Laura answered it, "Hello, Mr. Camper." Laura turned to John. "Mr. Camper wants to meet with you."

John's character instantly changed. He opened his eyes with excitement. "Give me the phone, sweetie."

"Hi, Mr. Camper. No, I cannot meet tomorrow. We will be in Santa Cruz this weekend after my meeting in Scotts Valley tomorrow morning." John listened. "Tonight? Yes, we can meet you there! Cheers."

"George Camper, whom I was telling you about, wants to discuss my business plan over dinner tonight. We are meeting him at eight. Let us plan to leave around seven-thirty?"

Laura nodded, grateful that he was feeling better and looking forward to something else, "You're going to impress him, Tiger." She was amazed by his sudden transformation; he had the wind in his sails and could see again.

**Folsom Intel Plant Conference Room**

Peter was seated at a conference table surrounded by a dozen technology reporters. He had propped his injured foot on another chair, studying the whiteboards that covered the room's walls and a projection screen. At the podium in the front of the room stood Intel's Vice President of Product Development. He was a narrow South Asian man in his mid-forties, wearing frameless glasses. He wore a gray suit with a green striped tie, and his voice had a monotone sing-song drone as he talked about a feature slide on the projection screen.

"I want to summarize the advanced features of our new Pentium Three chip. It has Universal Identifier, 3D acceleration, high-definition television, and e-commerce features." He said with an air of finality. The VP paused, somberly removing his glasses as he turned to face the room. He sighed heavily before beginning. "I regret to inform you Rupert Lee—a valuable design team member, was found slain in San Francisco last night. He would have reviewed his work with you on the Universal Identifier coding on the new chip. Now, I will answer what questions I can after our presentation."

He trailed off, striding over to the table to grab a stack of reports which he began distributing to the waiting reporters. "Please find the information on the chip in your white papers. Rupert's Indian wife has set up a fund for donations to their favorite charity, the Sri Ram Ashram, where he donated many computers and spent time training orphans in India. Thank you."

The briefing ended as the screen retracted into the ceiling. A mechanical hum in the background stopped, and reporters filed out of the room. The VP walked over as Peter limped to the door with his ornate seventeenth-century cane in his grasp.

Peter side-eyed him as he said in a quiet voice, "The universal identifier has some privacy rights groups alarmed. They are calling it a backdoor nightmare for government intrusion."

"The internet will be made more secure with a unique address," replied the VP.

Peter paused, lifting his right hand, and his unlatched cane's handle slid open to expose its sword.

The VP smiled, "I heard the pen is mightier than the sword, but I guess you like to have a backup."

Peter blushed, "Sorry about that. My grandfather gave it to me—I forgot to lock the handle. Now, about that backdoor?"

"Rupert's work just patched the very holes concerning them. It is very robust now. As you know, a unique machine identifier allows the best internet interaction, and the security needed for e-commerce." Peter knew a smooth answer when he heard one.

**Harry's Car**

Harry's XK8 was in immaculate condition, until now. Peter assailed the dashboard with discarded tissues, an Actifed package, and orange peels. Harry drove while Peter reclined in the passenger seat.

"Harry, thanks for driving. My foot's not feeling great," Peter's voice was thick.

Harry gave him a sidelong glance, "You look like shit warmed over."

"That good?" Peter gave a congested laugh, a stuffy sound leaving his mouth.

"You must follow up with Intel's Internet Network Operation center business."

Peter bowed his head, "Enough, Harry—I'm tired, but it's not like I got any sleep."

"Did you see anything about Rupert's death in the Chronicle?"

"No, I did not. Do you need me to read it to you?" Peter looked at him warily, tossing aside any notion of sleep for now.

"I did not have a chance to read the paper. How about the press release? What does it say?"

Peter straightened up to rifle through his bag and pulled out the briefing papers. He glanced over it quietly, his eyes widening in disbelief.

"Holy shit, Harry, I met him last night in Sacramento. I knew I had seen him somewhere before." Peter swallowed, fighting off a shudder. "I was there in San Francisco, where he died. I followed the limo I told you about into Pacific Heights."

Concern flashed across Harry's face, "The Chronicle is in the back seat, Peter."

Peter leaned over and grabbed the paper, eyes scanning the text in panic, "The police call-in number is listed."

"Call them, Peter."

Peter nodded, pulling out his phone and dialing the number.

"Lt. Joe Brick, please," Peter coughed, grabbing another tissue while he waited for the call to connect.

**Lt. Joe Brick's Office**

The lieutenant was exhausted. He wanted nothing more than to stretch but felt too stiff, and his face reflected his high fever. Steam wafted up from his brimming coffee cup of chicken soup next to a small pile of cough drops, discarded wrappers, Sudafed, and tissues on his desk. Joe looked at the framed photo of his daughter on his desk, where she was spelunking in a cave, as he sipped the hot soup.

He reached over to play his voicemails. He perked up at once, smiling as he listened to his daughter's voice message.

"Hi, Dad, I am going to Costa Rica to study bat caves next month. Steve's band has a record release party on Tuesday at the Utah club, just down the street from your office. Oh, and his hair is not purple anymore. Come over for the party at eight!"

Joe's soft smile faded, his eyes rolling as an embarrassing, painful memory flashed across his face. The next message was from his ex-wife, Meg.

"Hey, Brick, it's Meg. Can you get your stuff out of the garage? I need room for Jim's car; please rent a storage unit, will you? It's been two years already, for Christ's sake!"

Before Joe could dwell on his thoughts, the intercom crackled to life. "Brick, pick up, line one."

Joe coughed, picked up his phone, and answered with a gravelly voice. He listened quietly to the man on the other end, nodding and asking a few quick questions before ending the call. Lt. Brick pulled out the agent's card and dialed his number.

**Mike Murphy's FBI Office**

Mike and Tim Thompson, the Special Agent in Charge of the San Francisco Office, were conducting a debriefing on the pursuit and Rupert Lee's murder. Mike leaned back at his desk, nodding at Tim, leaning in the office doorway.

"Tim, we were lucky to track him yesterday," Mike said to his manager, who must have been in his early sixties. "Good move getting our vehicles fitted with large fuel tanks."

Tim Thompson was dressed in a white shirt, with his black and blue striped tie and collar loosened. "What do we know about Rupert Lee?" asked Tim.

Mike glanced at his notes, scratching his head as he lifted the page. "We know he was Intel's lead designer on its firmware chipset identifier."

"You're not a tech guy. Do you know what you just said means at all?" Thompson asked, making Mike frown.

"No, " Mike said with a little embarrassment, "but I'll find out."

Mike's cell phone rang, cutting their conversation short.

"I will let you get back to work. You still have another week before you retire," Tim said, turning around. "We're still on for dinner? I will buy it; you drive. I am going to get my coat."

Mike nodded, answering the phone as he did. "Hi, Lieutenant, give me a second." He pulled a file from his desk drawer, flipped it open, and picked up a pen. "What is the number? I owe you. I will check back in with you. Thanks."

He hung up the phone, pushed back his chair, and hustled to the doorway. He called out to Tim's retreating figure. "We got a break! Do you want to get my car while I call the lead?"

Tim turned around, catching Mike's tossed car keys. Mike returned to his desk, placing a call to the witness.

**Harry's Car**

Harry took the exit for Gilman at the Golden Gate Field's racetrack. Traffic had started backing up with the rush hour. They took the two-lane access road that wedges between the San Francisco Bay and the stalled bumper-to-bumper traffic on Highway 80. A thin fence separated them. There was a striking contrast between congestion on one side and an isolated jogging path on the other. Peter blew his nose into a wad of tissues again.

Harry glanced at him worriedly. "It sounds like it's getting worse."

"Don't expect me tomorrow," he said warily. "I'd better call off my date with George and Happy."

Peter pulled out his phone to call Happy but stared at a blank screen instead. He sighed, leaning his head against the headrest.

"My phone died."

"Almost there," Harry replied.

## Holiday Inn Emeryville

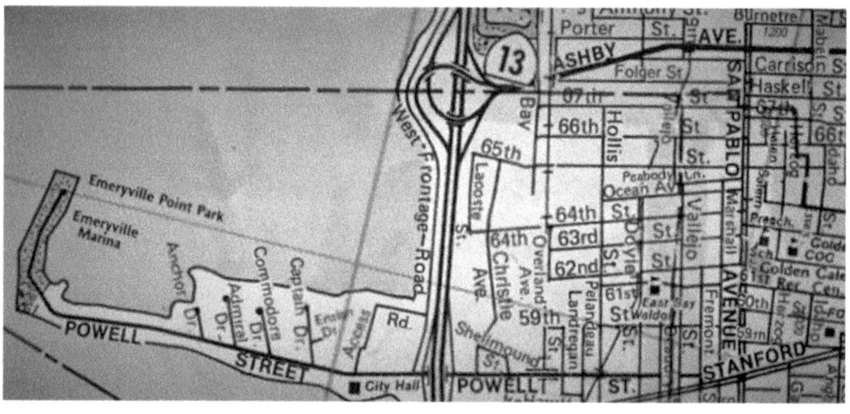


Harry's XK8 pulled into the parking lot. Peter hobbled out with his cane, uncomfortably walking the few steps to his car, and got in. He plugged his phone into the charger and waited for the phone to come to life.

He started the car, glancing down at a message before picking up the phone again to return the call.

"This is Peter Holland."

**Basement, FBI Building**

Mike exited the elevator with a file. His phone rang, stopping the agent in his tracks. "Special Agent Murphy here. Mr. Holland? I am glad you called. Can we talk tonight? I am in the city."

"I have a date at the Boulevard at eight. Can you meet me on the curb at Mission?" Peter responded.

"I know the place," Mike said.

Mike waved to Tim as he got into the car. Mike tapped his phone with his hand, and Tim waved back before closing the car door.

"How will I find you?" Mike asked, watching Thompson start his SUV. A massive explosion ripped the car apart, fling Mike to the ground. Mike scrambled back, anguish and horror riddling his features as he realized what had just happened.

Tim was gone. Mike leaned on one elbow, looking at the fiery remains of his friend.

"What the hell was that? Are you okay?" Peter asked.

"Someone just blew up my car," Mike said, sitting up. " The car I would've been in if you hadn't called."

Mike's head was reeling, and his ears were ringing. "Keep your eyes open, Peter. You do not know what you just walked into; I still want to see you at seven."

**Peter's Car**

Peter Holland sat still, stunned at the mayhem over the line.

"I will be in an older model silver Q45. Okay, see you in about thirty with traffic," he said.

Peter chugged the rest of his Dayquil before starting his car. He pulled out of the parking lot among the high-rise office and condominium towers juxtaposed with the mudflats of San Francisco Bay. He made a U-turn going east on Powell Street's landfill extension into the estuary. The Q45 accelerated on the ramp to the Bay Bridge.

**Jorge Esparante's Villa Guadalajara**

Jorge sat on his yellow silk Louis XVI couch, enjoying a scotch as salsa music played in the background. His cell phone rang, disrupting his enjoyment. Jorge answered.

"It is done. No way could he have survived the blast."

Jorge impassively listened before challenging Igor, who was on the other end of the line. "Are you sure it was the right car?"

"I tailed his car to the FBI building and placed the bomb underneath it myself. I watched the car door close and then triggered the package."

Jorge's lips curled into the ghost of a smile as he answered. "Sergei will take care of you."

**Boulevard Restaurant**

A cab pulled into the valet station at the white double entry doors to the restaurant. Happy's cobalt blue pumps touched the wet pavement, her black lace tights disappearing under a blue leather skirt. She clasped her matching blue Ferragamo purse as she pulled her trench coat closed over her dark green silk blouse and slid out of the cab and into the street. She walked across the curb into the brasserie.

The vaulted brick ceiling greeted her. Lampposts styled like French streetlights lit dark beams with blown glass lamp-shaded lights, branching off, painting the ceiling with indirect lighting.

The deep red, redwood bar had a low counter at the end for dining. The mosaic tile floor's blue peacock welcomed customers. The timeless La Belle Époque-inspired design flowed through the long room fenced with railings mimicking a Paris Street café.

Happy approached the vacant host station and saw an older, smiling Chinese man waving at her, clad in a dark suit and red tie. She strutted to the window booth near the bronze country maiden statue as he rose from his seat to greet her.

"Good evening, Ms. Camper," said General Chen. "I want to thank you for your helping China modernize out of the grass hut era."

"You are welcome, General Chen." Happy responded.

"China recovered from the Great Leap Forward only after Mao's death." General Chen solemnly spoke. "This new chip fabrication plant will allow China to build its computer infrastructure and help train our future engineers and scientists."

**Peter's Car**

Peter pulled up to the curb on Mission Street outside the Parisian-style three-story building with its fashionable mansard roof. The first-floor restaurant had blue canopies and columns framing white window casements.

A few minutes early, he looked through the restaurant windows and at once spotted Happy. He smiled at the sight of her. He saw her walk to a table with an older Chinese man through the restaurant. Peter turned on the radio, searching for a station that would better reflect his day.

**Boulevard Restaurant**

Happy and the General stood at the restaurant's interior transition from wood and barrel-vaulted brick ceilings to elaborate patterned tile floors, simple drywall vaults at the top, and decorative tile-wrapped posts.

General Chen beamed at Happy. "Thank you for taking one last meeting. My investors are anxious to conclude our business."

"I might want to take some time off after this merger closes," Happy responded, delighted.

"With your commission, it will be easy to do so," the General said brightly. "My country has much to thank you for, Ms. Camper."

"Do you mind if I freshen up?" Happy asked, glancing at the back of the room.

"No, no, not at all," the General waved dismissively. "Sergei is running late."

**Tim's SUV**

The pavement reflected the tall office towers crowding the street through the bomb-cracked windshield as the wipers cycled, and Mike drove down Mission Street. Tim's SUV's rearview mirror reflected his injured face, gashed from the shrapnel that had flown everywhere during the explosion. He held the phone to one ear.

"Peter, I am pulling up beside you. Jump in my car, and we will talk."

Peter hobbled out of his car and got into Mike's SUV. The engine was running, and Mike wheeled right onto the Embarcadero. The car slowed to a stop under the Bay Bridge, shrouded in rain and mist.

"Hello, Mr. Holland. I am Special Agent Mike Murphy."

## Boulevard Restaurant

Sergei's Mercedes pulled up to the valet station. The Russian climbed out the rear door, clad in a dark raincoat and hat. He stopped, surveying the area briefly. He narrowed his eyes, noticing Peter getting into a dark SUV. Sergei turned to the driver's lowered window.

"Follow that SUV," he commanded darkly.

## Tim's SUV

Mike kept his eyes on the road, reaching his hand out to shake. Peter declined the proffered hand, eyeing the cracked windshield warily. He studied the gashes on Mike's face quietly.

"You don't want to catch what I have," he stated. "For that matter, I am not happy being caught in this mess."

Mike's face was stoic. "Let's drive to PacBell Park and see how construction is going."

## China Basin at Third Street

PacBell Park's partially completed grandstands opened to China Basin. Mike pulled the SUV close to the curb next to the bridge operation shack for the Lefty O'Doul Bridge. The canal stood between them and the ballpark under construction. A passing limo's tires made a strange humming sound over the grated bridge surface.

The Park and the bridge over the canal were visible through the damaged windshield of the SUV. Rain dribbled down the cracks in the glass. Peter coughed, watching the black sedan pass them.

Mike turned to him, forcing a lighthearted opening. "You're right about me not wanting to catch what you have, Mr. Holland."

Peter nervously cleared his throat, feeling out of his element. He dreaded the impending conversation.

"Call me Peter, please," he tried. Peter gestured towards Mike's facial injuries. "What happened?" he asked.

Mike's expression turned serious. "I am getting too close to an international drug dealer, and the cartel has a contract on me, Peter. My regional director started my car while we were on the phone," he sighed heavily. "Better him than me, it blew sky high. Are you a reporter?"

He could talk shop. Peter nodded. "I work for *Upside*, a technology rag."

"I've seen it and read it," Mike followed an idle raindrop with his eyes. "Did you write the exposé on how cocaine was used for industrial espionage? That is why I am on this case," Mike said.

"Yes, that was mine. My editor was asking me for a follow-up. However, all my sources have dried up, or were fired, or were found dead."

"What can you tell me about Rupert Lee?" asked Mike.

"I met him briefly in Sacramento last night. He was with an imposing Russian gent with a limp, Sergei Marcov," Peter reported, feeling goosebumps at the mere thought of the Russian. "He makes the hairs on my neck stand up."

Mike had taken out a notebook and continued to scribble whatever Peter said. "What were you doing in Sacramento?"

Peter cleared his throat again. "I spent the day interviewing George Camper. His breakthrough in security encryption is making the news, and he testified at a security hearing at the Capitol." He turned in his seat to face Mike more fully. "Do you know the Russians are cyber-hacking the DoD?"

Mike met his gaze. "How did you wind up at the Baker Street Steps last night?"

"George had to stay for more meetings today, and his sister gave me a lift back to my car at a BART Station. I left my phone in her car and caught up with her at Skates in the Berkeley Marina," Peter paused, feeling a sneeze coming. He sighed when nothing happened. "Just a minute…." Peter wiped his nose before continuing, "Marcov walks into the restaurant as Happy, and I were walking to her car."

Mike raised an eyebrow, his lips turning up in a bemused smirk. "Did you say Happy?"

Peter's thoughts turned to her, feeling his shoulders at ease with mere reflections of her. "Yes, her name is Happy Camper. Her folks have a little twisted sense of humor."

Mike reached for his radio handset. "Meyers here. Joyce, find out all you can about George Camper and Happy Camper. Yes, I said Happy. H-A-P-P-Y. Thanks." He dropped the handset. "Go on, Peter."

"Happy has a significant merger going down, and being a reporter, I smelled a big story," he said. "I watched three people get out of Sergei's limo and into an SUV. Sergei came out of the restaurant just after Happy. She drove off, and I followed Sergei's SUV to the Baker Steps."

Mike stopped writing in his notebook.

Peter had fallen quiet. He shuddered suddenly. "I followed Rupert down the steps into the fog and heard choking sounds. Then this hulking guy with a buzzcut was coming up the stairs toward me."

"I was the guy at the top of the stairs," Mike said. "You nearly got yourself killed last night. I followed Marcov from Lake Tahoe yesterday as part of a drug deal. I saw you nearly get run over by his car in Sacramento."

Peter's eyes widened as he connected the dots.

"You were catching up to Ms. Camper," Mike said. "What do you know about the merger?"

"I can ask her in thirty minutes," he offered.

Mike nodded. "Just be careful, Peter," he said slowly. "Stop thinking about having kids with Happy and worry about what Sergei is doing."

Peter swallowed thickly. "You don't think Happy's involved?"

"Don't be so naïve," Mike said as if speaking to a teenager. "Don't you think Happy may be up to her neck in Lee's death?"

The radio crackled to life. "Mike, Happy Camper is a registered agent of the Chinese government. She arranged for an export license for chip fabrication technology.

Peter leaned back in his seat, quiet until he said, "I didn't know she was working for China."

"Thanks, Joyce. I owe you dinner!" Mike said. He turned to Peter. "What was Lee working on at Intel?"

"Lee just completed the chipset identifier firmware coding for their latest microprocessor. Intel's briefing discussed the security concerns with its unique machine identification."

"So let me get this straight," Mike finished writing something in his notebook. "Our dead man is Intel's expert on chip security. What is the scariest scenario?"

Peter's mind raced to the scariest thing he could imagine, then voiced it "Programmers always leave a backdoor to their coding. Scariest? How about a new chip plant producing counterfeit Intel chips used in network servers with built to order security holes about to be running the world's financial systems, infrastructure, and in our national labs?"

Mike glanced at his watch. "Peter, I'd better get you back to the restaurant."

Peter nodded, his thoughts racing. "You've got me fucking terrified."

Mike's SUV pulled up to the curb. Peter got out, briefly pausing when Mike leaned over.

"Try to keep her here for at least an hour," Mike said.

Peter nodded, his face grim. "I was looking forward to a long dinner with her. Not so much now."

Mike handed him his card. "Easy, Peter, we don't know which side she's on," he trailed off, pulling over to the curb next near Pete's car. "Watch your back, and I'll be watching it too."

Peter took the card, pocketing it. He limped toward his car in the rain. He glanced back at Mike once for reassurance and saw the agent nod affirmatively.

Peter got in his car and read Mike's card. He turned it over and over absentmindedly while watching Happy, the Chinese man, and Sergei meeting over dinner at a window table. Happy was laughing at something the Russian had said. Peter knew he was flirting with her shamelessly. The Chinese gentleman put a file into his briefcase.

"General Chen, we should discuss your licensing, George Camper's security software for the computer production," Sergei suggested.

"I am meeting with George tonight and will discuss the opportunity with him." Happy, cheerfully agreed. She motioned to the waiter with a check-signing motion. "Speaking of which, I'll get the check which will come out of the fees." The waiter took her credit card.

"I need to freshen up before I meet a new client of his." Happy slid out of the booth, and the men rose.

Sergei grasped her hand and kissed it. "Soon, we will be off the clock. I do want to discuss my plans for you."

"Sergei, you are relentless." Happy brushed off his latest parry with a chuckle. She turned on her heel and walked to the rear of the restaurant.

Sergei turned to General Chen and said, "Resolved."

"To a fish, a shiny lure is its last meal," Chen replied.

"You are right, Chen." As they walked out of the restaurant. "I must think of the perfect end for Ms. Camper; she knows too much about our dealings. If I cannot persuade her to come to our side."

**Peter's Car**

Peter took a stabilizing breath, feeling unwell and disturbed by his alarming conversation with Mike.

*Steady Peter, you are attracted to Happy, you can see her fitting into your life, and she is working on a merger that closed last night. But then, on the other side of the ledger, there are dead bodies, a KGB thug, a drug deal, and an FBI car bombing.* Peter thought to himself, reaching over to switch on the radio.

A blues song played a duet of a standup bass under a tenor flute. A whiskey-voiced man sang in a deep voice. Peter threw his head back against the headrest, glum with how well the song fits his mood.

*"I don't know what I'm going to do.*

*When I'm just thinking of you*

*I can't stand here being all alone.*

*I like you too much. I have to know.*

*I can't stand it. I can't make it.*

*What am I going to do?"*

The flute played a haunting solo. Peter watched Happy signal for the check. The waiter appeared at the table within moments, and she handed him a credit card. Happy got up from the table with the men, and Sergei kissed her hand before she headed to the ladies' room.

*"I don't trust you out with all of those guys.*

*Telling me you love me, but I have eyes.*

*You thought I was dumb, not too sharp.*

*You better watch it, babe; it's about who dies.*

*I can't stand it. I can't make it.*

*What am I going to do?"*

The men put their raincoats on.

Peter coughed violently, his back spasming from the pain.

The Russian checked his wristwatch as he and the Chinese gentlemen walked to the front door. Peter's thoughts drifted, unaware of Happy leaving the restaurant and approaching his car.

She knocked on his window. Peter jerked in surprise, noting her black trench coat tied loosely to her waist. Peter quickly reached over to let her in. He tossed the empty bottle of Dayquil in the backseat.

Happy studying him. "What are you doing out here, Peter?"

"Waiting for you."

**Sergei's Limo**

The Russian got into his car; eyes narrowed as he watched Happy get into Peter's car up the street. The rain grew heavier as he slid into the backseat.

"Comrade, I must alert you to a security threat." Boris turned to face him, his expression anxious. "Last night, at the Berkeley Marina, I saw that car when you met with Ms. Camper."

Sergei remained impassive. "I will drop you over to the Hyatt, Boris. Get a cab and follow Ms. Camper wherever she goes. I will drive back to the Consulate and report," his sights locked on Peter's car. "I cannot have Moscow thinking I am not doing my job. We have too many years into this to start relaxing."

**Peter's Car**

Happy looked over Peter closely. Her eyes narrowed in concern at his condition.

"Peter, you do not look so good. Are you feeling, okay?" She reached over to feel his forehead.

"No," he said. "I'm coming down with something I picked up last night at the ER."

Happy's brows furrowed. "ER?"

"I hurt my foot last night," he said, not bothering to go into specifics. He knew how close she was to him and his heart. Her scent wrapped him and embraced him, despite his stuffy nose.

"You're burning up," she tutted. "I'll drive you home—we'll cancel with my brother."

## Ninth & Lawton

The flame from a cigarette lighter illuminated the faces of two men sitting in a parked sedan across the street from John and Laura's cozy townhouse rental. Trimmed hedges stepped up the knoll to trees hiding the setback townhouses on their right. The Muni's electric lines ran above. John and Laura exited their townhouse and got into John's wagon.

Laura backed it out of the driveway and drove off. A dark sedan up the block started in pursuit while a second car remained.

Igor and Dmitri, the two men, got out of the remaining car and walked to the house. Dmitri, a large bald man, knelt and started to jimmy the lock. His hulking form contrasted with Igor's slimmer figure.

## Mike's SUV

Mike picked up Peter's discarded tissues and tossed them away, using hand sanitizer before reaching for his handset. He was parked a few spots up Mission Street from the Boulevard Restaurant.

"I need that second car," he said.

"Mike, I can only spare one car," Agent Parker said through the radio. "We have a major Op going down in Chinatown. We are about to go in."

Mike nodded. "Thanks, Paul. One car is better than none. I hope it is a slow night. My informant is about to leave. I will check in later."

"It's going down now," Agent Parker's voice cut out momentarily. "Go! Go! Go!"

**Mission Street**

A cab pulled up to the restaurant in the steady rain as Happy, and Peter swapped seats. The Ferry Terminal blocked the end of the street across the Embarcadero. Happy drove off, turning right onto the Embarcadero, unaware of the cab that followed them. Mike pulled out and turned right onto Stuart Street.

Happy and Peter drove past Stuart and up toward Howard.

Mike's car was at the corner of Stuart and Howard. The Bay Bridge dominated the horizon. He almost followed Peter's car just as the same cab drove by. Mike spotted Boris in the back seat.

Peter's car left behind the waterfront and drove up the hill between the mid-rise office buildings. Peter recognized her approach to the bridge.

"Hey, you know your way around," he said stuffily.

Happy smirked. "Around what, Peter?"

Peter rolled his eyes. "Around downtown, Happy."

"I know my way around," she continued honestly. "I put myself through UC part-time as a bike messenger my first year. That is when the finance bug bit me."

She brushed her hair out of her eyes.

"As I ended my shift. A Goldman Sachs manager needed to add one page to the report. I stood around listening to him on the phone, getting the last part of a deal down," she turned to Peter with a whimsical smile. "I said to myself, 'I can do this.' The next day, I changed my major from Eastern Symbolism to Economics and a minor in Chinese."

Happy turned onto First Street, her lips still curved in a nostalgic smile. "I was recruited out of college by a Sacramento lobbying firm. I lived with Aunt Em, spent two years on how the law was made, and started putting deals together. Then Sand Hill Road called, and now I am here."

Peter arched his eyebrows. "Impressive. So, can you tell me about your big deal?" He watched her guardedly, like a mouse in a cat's paws.

"Peter! I am under an NDA," she answered. "Do you want me to kiss and tell?"

"Yes!" Peter countered.

Happy drove past a 76-gas station on the right as traffic slowed before merging onto the Bay Bridge ramp.

**Boulevard Restaurant Entrance**

John's dented wagon pulled into the valet station. John got out, dressed in a sports coat and dark slacks, walked around Laura's door, and opened it. Laura, in a green wrap dress and raincoat, gave John the keys. John tossed the keys to the valet.

"I treasure this car. Take extra loving care of it," he said jokingly, motioning to the cracked windshield. The valet gaped at the car and shook his head.

George Camper sat at the bar, reading the Chronicle. His eyes darted up as John and Laura approached to greet him.

"John and Laura," he rose from his seat. "I am glad you could make it. I invited my sister and friend to dinner, but they just canceled. I hope you are hungry."

"It's a pleasure to meet you, Mr. Camper," Laura smiled.

"Call me George, please."

An attractive young hostess approached the trio with menus in her hand. "Mr. Camper, your table is ready. Please follow me."

**Ninth and Lawton**

The living room was in shambles. Papers from the desk were scattered over the floor, sofa cushions had been cut open, and books disarrayed in the bookcase. Igor was going through John's home laptop, as his rain-soaked hair dripped onto his face and glasses. His face was waxen, his thin hands inserting each CD into the computer as he scanned the contents. He dialed Sergei on his mobile phone.

"I have his computer and disc drive binder," he said.

Sergei was seated in Vulakovich's chair, a vodka bottle and glass in front of him. A cigarette hung from his lips, the end aglow. A locked file cabinet drawer was open, with a file lying on top.

"What are you telling me, Igor?" Sergei's voice was ice-cold. "You have the disc, or you don't?"

Igor slid the last disc into the computer. His voice trembled as he reported. "The computer disc is not here. I have looked at every computer file. Nothing. And we thoroughly searched the house."

Igor stilled as he listened to Sergei on the other end.

"Okay, okay, okay," he nodded, signaling to Dimitri. The two men finished their work and left the house with John's laptop and stereo receiver.

**General Chen's Room**

Steady rain pelted the window of General Chen's room as he intently studied the expansion map of Shanghai's Pudong New Area. The map was the architectural plan for the microprocessor plant and designs for a vast, mid-rise office building.

His phone rang. Chen took a sip from the glass of Baijiu before he answered. He was expecting this call from Lieutenant Colonel Zhang Wei, his second in command.

"So, we are certain the PC plant is on schedule—and the microprocessor plant?"

Chen listened, and a thin smile of satisfaction took over his features.

"Even better," Chen answered, his voice suddenly sharp and commanding. "Your next focus will be on Oak Ridge National Lab as we discussed. I want to know about this abandoned reactor design called a Molten Salt Reactor and their Thorium cycle research. Our environmental movement funding has helped shut down nuclear power plants in the West.

Our American friends, with their NRC and EPA restrictions on mining rare earth elements due to their Thorium and Uranium content because they are considered source material for nuclear weapons. Our national supply chain policy forces capitalists to build factories in China, allowing them to source our rare earth components and alloys. They are giving us a perfect monopoly and consequently must share their designs and intellectual property with local partners. Please do not fail me and China, Colonel Zhang."

He ended the call, glancing at the screen as it rang again. This time, it was Sergei.

**Peter's Car**

Happy merged on the on-ramp and checked over her shoulder for traffic. She accelerated across two lanes of traffic between a bus and a tractor-trailer into a free lane.

Happy's maneuver suddenly cut off the taxi's pursuit of the car. The cab almost crashed into a bus that was merging onto the bridge. Boris leaned forward.

"If you would please not get us killed," Boris said to the cab driver.

"You did want me to follow that car, didn't you?" the driver asked.

Boris's phone rang suddenly. He answered.

"Da, da, yeah, yeah."

Ahead, Happy looked over to Peter, her eyes sparkling playfully.

"So, where to, gimpy?"

"Take eighty to the Emeryville-Powell exit, up to Hollis, and make a right. You must..."

"Cutover fast?" Happy smiled with in-control satisfaction. Peter gave in.

"I give up," he laughed. "You've got it handled."

"About time you started to see how capable I am," she laughed briefly before turning to Peter and saying in an almost motherly tone. "I will nurse you back to health, so leave it to me. What did you do to your foot?"

Happy cutover four lanes to make the Powell Street exit. Peter grimaced at the intense maneuver.

The cab followed the radical maneuver onto the off-ramp. A Honda Accord spun out of control on the wet pavement, barely avoiding the taxi, and crashed. Mike's SUV, following the cab, cleared the spinning car just in time and found the off ramp.

Peter grimaced at Happy. "I was in the ER last night, and I don't want to be there tonight," he cautioned, communicating his concern about Happy's driving.

"Like an idiot, I left my floor heater's key in the vent and jammed my toe into the key last night. It took ten stitches in the web of my foot. And, yes, it hurt. My booby prize was catching this cold."

Happy scrunched her face as she turned right onto Powell. "Ouch."

Mike was watching attentively, the taxi now four cars ahead of him, turning onto Powell Street following Peter's SUV.

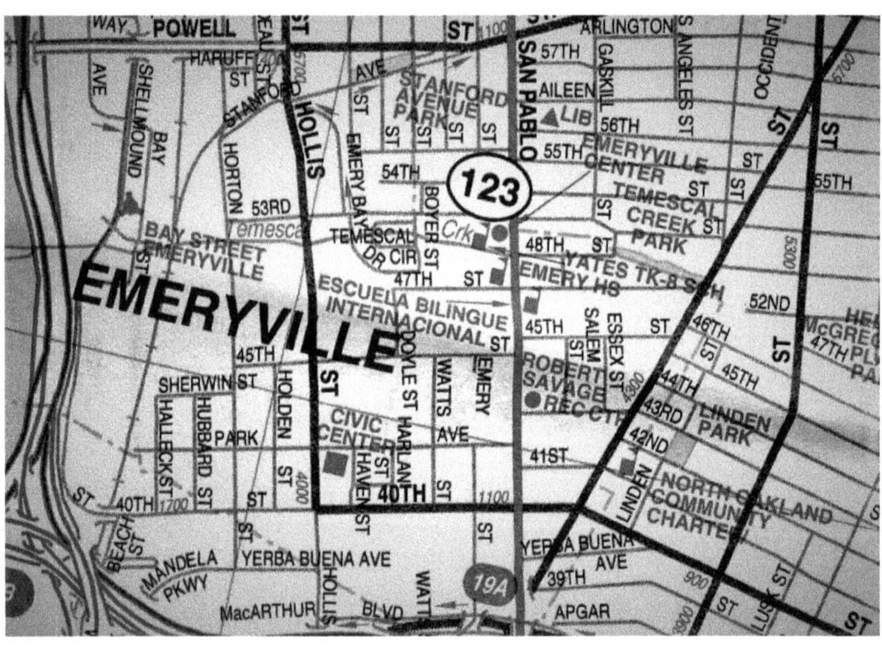

"Take Hollis and another right on the 45th. Then, down to the end, turn left and park."

Happy nodded. "Okie dokie artichokie."

Peter eyed her warily. "Why are you so nice to me?"

She shrugged. "Well, Peter, now the problem is the Nightingale Factor. Am I taking pity on you, like I would with anyone who gets hurt, or do I like you? What do you think?"

"How am I going to tell which way it is?" he asked.

"Peter," she smiled perkily. "I'll just have to keep you guessing."

Peter watched her turn onto Hollis. "Park behind that yellow Fiat."

"I see a Fiat, but there's too much dirt to tell what color it is," Happy noted.

"The artist who owns it isn't concerned with washing her car when a suitable art installation costs more than her car," he said.

"You did say there are many artists around here?"

"I live across the street," he reported. "Do you mind handing me my cane behind my seat?"

Happy reached behind the passenger seat and grabbed the baroque cane with the carved ivory handle.

"What an exquisite piece. How did you come upon it?" Happy asked appreciatively.

"I broke my leg in sixth grade, and my grandfather, who collected canes worldwide, thought I needed some help getting around."

**Hollis and 45th Street**

The cab pulled up alongside a converted warehouse, just out of sight of Peter's car. Boris exited the cab and crossed the street as the taxi drove away.

Mike pulled up to the corner slowly. The PG&E Electrical Transformer shop dominated the block; on the corner, topping the three roll-up door arches were bas-relief sculptures of a man, tools, and transformers, made by local public artist Scott Donahue. Mike watched Boris exit the cab and cross the road. Mike backed up his truck and parked.

Mike reached over for the radio. "Joyce, Mike. I need an address for Peter Holland. H-O-L-L-A-N-D, yes, as in Tulips. I will hold, yes, in Emeryville. Okay. Thanks."

"Mike, should I move up?" the FBI tail guy asked.

"Flattop left his cab on 45th street and is on foot. Circle over to Park and Horton," Mike said.

Mike left his car and walked around the corner of 45th. The streetlights reflected in puddles from the continuous downpour.

The steady rain drenched Happy and Peter. Large raindrops slanted through the entrance lamp above as he unlocked the small entry door in the big green loading door of the Artist Co-op. Peter held the smaller door open for Happy.

"Happy, my loft is on the left. Let's use the ramp," Peter motioned to the ramp on the left side of the loading dock. His limp was getting worse. They reached the double green doors of Peter's loft. Peter handed Happy his cane as he unlocked the door and opened it.

"My abode, fair maiden. Let me get the lights."

Happy grinned, handing him his cane. "Your sword, my Liege."

"It was given to me by a great grand wizard to slay dragons and demons. I am ready to battle for your honor," Peter pulled the sword out of the cane. Happy tilted her head, amused.

"Should I close my eyes while thou will'st slay your foes, my lord?"

Peter entered the loft, and the lights came on.

"Hither, fair maiden."

Peter scabbarded the sword into the cane and took a deep bow before waving her into his loft.

Happy entered with pageantry and gazed over the walls covered with Peter's artwork. She broke out of the mock role.

"I love your art, Peter."

Peter was in the kitchen, pulling out a bottle of wine.

"I'd pick up an odd piece here and there, and soon you are out of wall space," he shrugged. "It doesn't hurt to have a sister in the business—would you like a glass of wine?"

Happy looked over at him, smiling. "Yes, please. I will open it. But first, let's get you off your feet."

# Rain

As Mike Murphy walked up 45th Street, the rain thickened. Meanwhile, Boris crouched by Peter's Co-op's entry lock. He picked at it stealthily until a small, satisfied smile appeared when the latch released.

Outside the Boulevard Restaurant, a man in a black knit cap sat inside a dark sedan. He lit a cigarette and watched John and George through his small binoculars.

"You have a very well-thought-out business plan, John. I would have liked to have seen your presentation," George said as he pulled the disc from the folder and handed it back to John. "Here is the disc you gave me. Where did you get it? It is not your business plan."

John and George exchanged discs.

"The day I met you, I ran a video conference for Sergei Marcov, a Russian," John began. "His video card wasn't working, so he used my laptop's DVD player, and the discs somehow got mixed up."

John looked over at his fiancée as she stifled a yawn. "I have an early day tomorrow, a consult in Scotts Valley with Borland. The plan could start by picking up the lease on their now cast-off VTC systems," he said, hoping to wrap things up soon.

"That will make your numbers even better, John. We should be able to close on Tuesday." George said, pleased at the idea.

"Then, after Borland, we'll be off to Carmel before the weekend traffic." John continued.

"Sounds like a great weekend indoors," George said as they finished their dinner. "The jet stream will kick this storm down to Santa

Cruz tonight. I will review your plans this weekend and call you on Tuesday."

John nodded as he got up, helping Laura with her chair. "Tuesday is great, George. Thanks for a fine dinner."

"It was a pleasure meeting you, Mr. Camper," Laura said, a brief smile her farewell as she walked to the exit with John.

George motioned for the bill.

Andrei Laskin in the sedan outside spoke into his phone, describing George and John's actions as he looked through the binoculars, reporting their every move.

**Peter's Loft**

Happy was in the kitchen, taking the kettle off the stove and brewing tea. Her eyes traveled over the artwork in the loft once more, admiring the variety that adorned the walls. Sitting comfortably on the sofa, she sipped her wine while talking to Peter.

Happy pointed to one sizeable pastel-framed piece. "What is the large pastel print? Is it a pig in the seagrass, or what looks like one?"

"My sister did that piece years ago and gave it to me for Christmas," Peter said.

"Oh, I didn't intend it in a mean way," Happy said quickly.

Peter's lips lifted in a smile. "It looks like a bleached whale's skull to me." He looked over at Happy. "My joke is, I come from an artistic family, but I'm autistic."

Happy snickered as she walked over to the couch with a large mug of hot tea.

"Let's elevate that leg, Peter." Happy motioned his leg with her head. "Have some tea. I put honey and lemon in it. It should help with the cough."

"Which one?" Peter asked sheepishly.

"Cute, Peter. Your injured leg or your neglected leg?" Happy tilted her head quizzically. She saw the way Peter's eyes widened comically for a moment. "You are blushing. No matter how hard I tried, I did not think you would ever blush."

"You've succeeded at hard," Peter said. It was Happy's turn to blush, and her gaze softened. "How come there is no man in your life, Happy?"

"I'm in the middle of so many deals," Happy shrugged. "I have rules and do not mix business with pleasure. And do you know what?"

"What?"

"It gets lonely. Not that I am complaining," Happy smiled wryly. "It's difficult to meet a man that likes a similar variety of topics and art, with whom I'm not already in a business deal."

"Do you mind telling me about your current deal?" he arched an eyebrow as he looked up at her. "Or will that make it business between us?"

Happy smirked as she placed her wine glass on the coffee table. "It all depends on if I kiss you before or after I tell you, Peter."

Peter grabbed Happy's wrist and gently pulled her down to him.

**Boulevard Restaurant**

Laskin in the dark sedan started his car as he watched George Camper pay the bill at the restaurant.

**Horton Loft Entry**

Mike approached the entrance door. The door was ajar. Mike entered, the door creaking behind him as the wind whipped it closed with a loud thump. The sound of heavy rain pounding against the skylight covered Mike's footfalls.

He looked down at a long, expansive atrium, ears straining to catch a sound that would alert him to Boris' presence.

Boris was at Peter's door, quietly screwing a silencer on the gun. He heard the entry door close and turned his head at the sound.

Mike tiptoed up the worn ramp on the left of the loading dock, peering around the potted trees as he moved into the building. He felt a chill move up his spine.

Boris raised his gun as he backed away from Peter's door. He moved stealthily around the pools of light, waiting for the intruder.

Mike reached Peter's door. Boris holstered his gun in the shadows, pulling out his Russian NR-40 combat knife. He held the ricasso and black wooden handle of the 152 mm blade, with the edge upward as the Soviet Army trained him.

**Ninth and Lawton**

John and Laura pulled into their garage as the rain continued, pounding on the street. The couple walked arm-in-arm up the steps to the front door.

A dark sedan turned onto Ninth Street at the uphill corner. The driver parked, with the headlights off.

**Peter's Loft**

Boris saw Mike from the shadows. As the rain leaked through the roof into dozens of buckets, pots, and pans around the entire atrium, the steady drips splattered in an unsettling cadence. Boris tossed some loose change across the hallway.

Mike's head snapped around at the sound. Mike drew his gun and turned on his flashlight, moving toward the sound. He knew the man was here somewhere but not were.

Boris ducked into a hallway to avoid detection, but in his rush, he tripped loudly over a rain bucket, making water flood the floor. He cursed under his breath and ran down the narrow hallway.

Mike's flashlight traced Boris's flight down the darkened hallway. The agent warily followed his route to the communal showers on the right and noted the exit door on the left. The hallway was empty, and unfinished with overspray and splatters of dried plaster. Mike checked each shower stall with the flashlight and headed for the fire exit.

## The rear of the Loft Building

The outer wall of the rear patio led to the left. A cat leapt over a discarded sculpture on the ground, alerting Mike. He stopped on the patio, not liking the shadows beyond. Something surprised the cat. Mike turned on his heel and reentered the building.

Boris lurked in the shadows, knife at the ready. "He couldn't have known I was here," Boris said to himself. "Tonight, you are lucky, Mr. Agent Man."

The Russian reluctantly sheathed the blade, walking away from the building toward Holden Street.

## Ninth and Lawton

John and Laura stepped into their home, freezing at the sight that greeted them when he turned on the lights, and the couple stood still in shock at the mayhem before them.

"Stay here," John instructed, picking up a baseball bat he left near the front door. John swung it, his movements slow and cautious as he explored the first floor.

"Call the police," he whispered before heading upstairs.

Laura nodded; her eyes wide with panic as she dialed 911.

She described the state of their living room. Sofa cushions ripped apart; filling scattered over the floor. Drawers had been pulled open and emptied, their contents everywhere. Laura reported the situation and stayed put, worried about what sight would greet her if she dared to explore.

"John?" she called out cautiously just as her fiancé made his way back down.

"All clear." He put the bat down. "What did the police say?"

"They're on their way."

Later, John and Laura stood in their foyer, talking to a young police officer in a raincoat. Laura watched a CSI technician with a coffee-stained white shirt attempt to lift fingerprints off the front doorknob.

"Henry, no prints. They were wearing gloves," the technician reported. "There were pick marks on the lock."

"Thanks, Jerry. You can take off," the officer said before turning back to John and Laura, his raincoat dripping on their wood floor. "So just a stereo and a laptop are missing?"

The couple nodded.

"You're lucky. Typically, it is a smash-and-grab, with your front door kicked in," the officer said. "Here's my card if you find anything else missing."

John took the offered card as the police officer tipped his dripping plastic-covered cap and left through the front door.

The police officer got into his cruiser, pulling a U-turn on Ninth, and sped away, turning on his red light and siren as he left. John closed the front door before he could see a dome light appear in the sedan parked up on the rain-soaked street.

**John and Laura's Bedroom**

Laura was lying on her stomach, naked in their king-sized bed. propped up on their large, green, flannel-covered pillows.

"John, come back to bed," she called out. "Honey, I want you."

John replied from outside. "I just wanted to finish cleaning up the mess down here. I want to spend extra time in the morning with you."

Laura smiled, "I like the sound of that."

She bent her right leg up, her toes pointing as she stretched. John entered the room. He stood in the doorway, admiring her. Laura's gaze fixed on the engagement ring on her left hand.

"When are you coming back to bed?" she asked.

John ran from the door to the bed and dived in. Laura giggled.

"Stop looking at your ring," John said, his voice losing its teasing lilt as he kissed her. Laura wrapped her arms around his neck, letting her fiancé press her into the mattress as he climbed over her.

# Day Four

### John and Laura's Bedroom

John walked into the bedroom with coffee, eggs, toast, and the Chronicle tucked under his arm. Dawn broke through the darkness outside their window.

"Rise and shine beauty," he said softly, rousing his fiancée from her slumber.

### Peter's Bedroom

Peter was troubled by Happy's involvement with Sergei, but as true to his nature, he rarely denied himself female companionship. He clenched his hand in Happy's mussed-up hair, deepening their kiss. Happy let a soft moan escape her as she pulled the sheets up and around them. They were oblivious to the world.

### John's Car

Laura drove John's wagon to the meeting. They took the beautiful Junipero Sierra Freeway past Stanford's campus and its large radio telescope into San Jose. Laura managed the twisting turns of

Highway 17 over the summit at Patchen Pass and down into Scotts Valley.

**Peter's Bedroom**

Happy let her phone ring a couple more times before breaking the kiss with a scowl at the interruption. She reached over, rolling her eyes as she glanced at the name on screen. Peter waited for her to decide.

"It's George," she said before answering. "George, I am sorry Peter, and I had to cancel. Did you get my voicemail?"

"Yes, I did, Happy. I wanted to ask you about your deal with Sergei Marcov," George got straight to the point.

Happy arched an eyebrow, meeting Peter's curious gaze.

"You're the second man I care about who's asking me the same thing," she said as she lay back in Peter's arms. "I'll put you on speakerphone."

"I had dinner with John Nord about his video network deal," George's voice crackled through the speaker. "I was going to introduce him to you last night. His collateral included a presentation disc that got mixed up with Sergei Marcov's from a video conference he managed a few days ago at the Hyatt."

"How strange," she mused. "I was on that call."

"There's more—there's an advanced Intel chip design on it that shouldn't be in the hands of a Russian."

Peter straightened up. The light rain softly tinkling on the windows sounded through the loft. His head cast a shadow on the wall by the reading light. Suddenly, there was a knock on the door.

"George, this was not part of my deal. It was for a microprocessor plant for China's domestic market," Happy replied as she sat up and reached for Peter's shirt. "Talk to Peter while I answer the door."

Happy rose from the bed, and Peter's gaze followed her as she put on his shirt and fluffed her hair. She walked down the stairs to the door and looked briefly at herself in the mirror before opening the door.

"Hi, I'm Special Agent Mike Murphy with the FBI," Mike introduced himself, holding up his Badge and ID. "Is Peter in?"

"Yes, he is. He is on the phone right now." Happy answered.

"I want to speak with you and Peter about Sergei Marcov."

"Please come in," Happy invited as she stepped aside, opening the door wider. "My brother is on the phone with Peter, and they are just talking about Sergei."

Mike stepped through the door.

"Peter, you better come down here!" Happy called out. She gestured Mike over to the couch.

Peter hobbled down the stairs in a bathrobe, leaning on his cane. He joined Mike on the sofa, elevating his leg on the ottoman. He held Happy's phone on the other hand, George's voice still coming from the speakerphone.

"Hi, Mike," Peter said.

"Peter, do you know Special Agent Murphy?" Happy asked with a troubled look.

"I met him last night," Peter answered her.

"George, I'm with Mike Murphy, an FBI agent," Peter interrupted. "I was at a briefing yesterday at Intel. Did you know their chip ID designer, Rupert Lee, was killed the night before in San Francisco?"

Happy's eyes widened in shock as she turned to look at Peter.

"I introduced you to him at Paragary's last night, Peter," Happy said quietly.

Peter nodded. "I recognized him from his session at COMDEX last year. I never knew his name."

Mike watched the exchange before interjecting, "Mr. Camper, is there anything I should know?"

"I want to know why a Russian has Intel's chip design," George said. "John Nord gave me a business plan with a presentation on a CD. It somehow got mixed up with Marcov's disc. I gave John the disc back, but I made a bitmap copy."

Mike stood up, opening his coat to retrieve his notebook.

"Mr. Camper, I need to meet with you as soon as possible," he said, scribbling something on the page. "How early can you see me?"

"Why don't you come to my place now?" George asked. "I'm in lower Pacific Heights on California."

"I'll write down his address for you, Mr. Murphy." Happy wrote George's address on a slip of paper from her purse.

"I'll see you then," Mike replied.

"Great, see you then. I better call John Nord and warn him." George ended the call.

Mike walked to the front door, then said to the couple, "Ms. Camper, Peter, you must keep our discussion confidential." He warned them before leaving.

**George Camper's Study**

George ended the call, his expression becoming serious as he took in the added information they had just shared. He had to call John Nord. George leaned back in the leather chair, rocking it as he thought of what to do, making it creak loudly. The creak of his leather chair masked the sound of someone opening the door to his study.

"John, this is George Camper. Please call me back as soon as possible." George left a voicemail.

**Borland Software Scotts Valley**

Laura pulled into the empty parking lots of Borland Software in time for John to have his meeting.

"Great driving, babe!" exclaimed John.

John kissed Laura before getting out of the car. He turned to wave at her before walking into the building.

John checked his voicemail and made a call. "Hi, Mr. Camper. Can I call you right back?"

**George Camper's Study**

George's phone rings, and he answers it on his speakerphone. "Hi, Mr. Camper. Can I call you right back? I am going into a meeting at Borland now." John said.

"Yes, John. Please call back as soon as possible." George ended the call as he heard the study door closing. Turning his head, he saw a sizeable, broad man with a flattop enter the room.

"Yes, Mr. Camper, we will wait with you for John's call back." Said Boris. George was suddenly grabbed by his shoulders from behind by Andrei Laskin and forced back into his chair. Andrei held him down on the chair.

"We want the disc," Boris said menacingly.

"I don't know what you are talking about." George bravely replied.

"Mr. Camper, you were seen with John Nord last night in the restaurant exchanging the disc. Let us not make this more unpleasant than necessary. Yes?"

"All I have discussed with John Nord is financing his video teleconference startup. His presentation is on my desk in the manilla envelope." John strives to change the focus of the discussion.

Boris walked over to the desk and opened the envelope. He examined the contents, took the disc from its sleeve, turned to George's desktop, and inserted it. The computer came alive with the Secure Video Teleconferencing Network LLC. Presentation.

**Borland Software Scotts Valley**

A charcoal gray Audi sedan driven by the Siberian called Dimitri pulled into the entryway of the Borland parking lot far from the building. Dimitri was Sergei's most experienced and deadly driver. In the passenger seat was a bigger man named Lev. He had thick knuckles and massive hands—and knew his business.

## Borland Conference Room

John discussed an equipment leaseback with two of Borland's executives at the conference table.

"Thank you for this opportunity to pick up the lease on your video conference systems," John said. "This will be a tremendous help to my new conference company. I will bring the offer to my investor on Tuesday and close with you by the end of the week."

He stood, shaking hands with the two men, left the room, and walked to the lobby. He checked his phone, and it was low on power; he forgot to plug it into the charger in the car. John called George Camper back.

## George Camper's Study

Boris dialed his cell phone and ordered, "Take her."

George broke free of Andrei Laskin and reached for the phone as Boris stabbed him in his liver with his blade. The doorbell rang, followed by a light knock on the door. A pool of black blood formed on the carpet as Boris cleaned the blade on George's shirt.

"Let us go now." Boris walked to the front door and opened it to Mike Murphy.

"You're not George Camper?" Mike asked. "Who are you?"

"No, I am not Mr Camper. I just finished my interview with him," Boris answered pleasantly. "He is in his study, ill with a side ache. Good day." Boris and Andrei walked down the hallway to the elevator.

Mike was puzzled and entered the flat.

George's mobile phone rang, and Boris answered it. "We want the disc."

**Borland Software Scotts Valley**

John exited the building with a satisfied smile at the end of a successful meeting. He pulled out his phone and called George Camper. He was alarmed by the strange voice answering George Camper's phone.

Two men instantaneously exited the Audi as it pulled behind John's car. John froze as he saw them pulling Laura out of his car, forcing her into the back of the sedan.

"Laura!" he yelled, breaking into a run.

The sedan sped out of the parking lot, turning left onto Santa's Village Road. John yelled out in rage as he started the Taurus, then raced off after the Audi.

John's phone rang, and he answered it. "We want the disc, or else your pretty is dead." rasped the voice. "Go home, and we will call you." The line went dead.

## Peter's Loft

Peter lounged on the couch, a steaming mug of coffee in his hand as his gaze skimmed over the first page of the Chronicle. The morning sun streamed through the skylights, bathing the loft in amber light. He wondered about Happy and her connection with Sergei.

Happy let herself in the door, dressed in Peter's bathrobe, with her dark hair up in a towel. Peter smiled.

"Peter, if we are going to keep seeing each other, we have to do something about the showers," Happy said seriously, undoing the towel and combing out her hair. "I was in the shower, and someone had the worst bowel movement. It was incredible. I almost called 911."

Peter snorted. "Oh, that's Maurice. He is a legend in the bowels of this building."

"Ew!" Happy exclaimed, holding her nose as she glared at Peter's reflection in the mirror.

Peter's phone rang.

"Hello?" Peter answered. "Hi, Mike."

He listened to the FBI agent's grim message before gesturing at Happy to join him on the couch.

**George Camper's Study**

Mike stood over George as the EMTs worked on George. The books in his study were scattered all over the floor. The overturned room had John's open proposal sitting on his desk, with the disc removed.

"Peter, I have bad news. Is Happy there?" Mike sighed. "Tell her to sit down."

Mike swallowed, eyes darting about the study for more clues.

"They attempted to kill George," he told them. "Luckily, I got here when I did. The EMTs are working on him, but he might not make it. Be careful."

**Peter's Loft**

Peter heard a noise at the door and hobbled over to investigate. Outside, Igor jimmied the lock, then burst through the front door, his gun out. Seeing the weapon, Peter stood in the hallway, calming his breathing. He pulled the sword from his cane, letting the sheath clatter to the floor. Igor was surprised by the noise and when he glanced down, Peter thrust the blade forward into his side.

The gun went off, and the sound of the silencer chunked as the bullet sailed past Happy, lodging itself in the pastel art piece on the wall. Peter slashed wildly at Igor's hand, making him drop the gun. He tackled Igor, wrestling him to the floor, sending the gun sliding across the floor.

Happy picked up the gun as it clattered against her feet. Igor had Peter in a chokehold, and the two men struggled on the floor, straining to overpower each other. Peter's grip on his sword loosened, and Igor tried to stab Peter in the neck with a knife.

Happy aimed, and with a silent prayer, she fired. Igor slumped back, and Peter struggled out of his grasp.

"Happy—you shot him!"

Happy shrugged, the gun still in her hand.

"You killed him first."

**Felton Empire Road Curve**

The monsoon gale lashed at the deserted sweeping curve. The rain was relentless, the air making guttural, multi-tonal sounds as the redwoods bent in the heavy wind. Branches snapped as billions of needles rained down.

John's faded blue Taurus wagon veered dangerously on the wet asphalt. His expression set in a grim line as he drove as fast as his wagon would go. He left Highway 17 on Mount Herman Road.

*"It is Santa Cruz classic rock. It is a wonderful day to stay indoors with another classic from Yes, Owner of a Lonely Heart."*

# The Chase

The song on the radio played, with the DJ speaking between the lyrics, about reports of the weather and torrential rain, breaking the rock song into segments. John sped past the cars on the highway, his eyes searching desperately for the Audi.

"We have a breaking story. There is a national weather alert for the Santa Cruz Mountains, torrential rain for the next six hours. Now, back to Yes."

*"Move yourself."*

John's blue Taurus wagon approached the last stoplight leaving town. The light turned green, and John's car jerked forward, passing five cars ahead at the intersection as the road narrowed to two lanes uphill.

The dark Audi pulled away from the fuel tanker, slowly moving uphill and disappearing into the rain. John's foot pressed down on the gas pedal as if that would somehow make his car go any faster. The rain slowed his progress as he watched the sedan cruise uphill in the torrential rain, in perfect view but too far ahead of him.

The wind and rain grew more intense, gaining a hurricane-like strength and covering the road's shoulder with mud and debris as trees bent from the force of the wind.

John's wagon swerved back into the lane after passing a tanker truck. His movements were rash, and the wagon barely missed a collision with the big rig, whose air horn blared in protest.

John paid no attention to the loud horn behind him. His eyes darted up as he frantically checked his mirrors. He reached for his phone, pressing the side button frantically, hoping it would power on.

He cursed under his breath, looking around for the charger. He spotted it on the far side of the dash, sliding off and thudding onto the floor in front of the passenger seat as his car veered back into the lane. The truck's horn faded into the distance, the rain pelting against the windshield mercilessly.

John turned the wipers to their highest setting, struggling to see through the heavy rain blowing sideways into the hillside, the redwoods groaning and cracking from the wind. The blue Taurus wagon battled the steep incline. John's heart hammered as the Audi slipped out of sight. His wagon barely made it up the steep slope when he spotted the sharp curve ahead. He gritted his teeth, jaw clenching as the car slid into the turn. He did everything he could to keep the vehicle on the curve as the road entered Felton.

John's car came to a rolling stop at Gramhill Road. He turned right in hot pursuit of the sedan. He crossed Highway 9 and went onto Felton Empire Grade at suicidal speed. Several cars spun out of control on the slippery roads. John sped past them, his car veering in and out as he arrived on Felton Empire Road. The forest canopied the road, giving him a slight respite from the chaotic downpour.

A sign announcing the speed limit, 15 mph, leaned to the left as the weight of the hillside gave way. The road had become almost impassable as raging elements tore large branches onto the road and car. The canopy above prevented heavy downpours, but the howling wind driving the storm was relentless.

Hairpin turns awaited John. The road thrust up to the right and zigzagged in a series of climbing loops. The eroded shoulder opened to the ravine below. The pavement ascended into the redwoods. John swallowed, his knuckles turning white on the steering wheel as the wagon disappeared around the turn with the sweeping wakes of water.

Finally, the road straightened out into more manageable, rhythmic curves. John increased his speed, the rock song ending as he approached the yellow speed limit sign.

Frustrated, John turned off the radio, his eyes searching desperately for the Audi. His car drifted through the hairpin curve, racing around the sweeping blind bend as the hillside above gave way, the mud and debris sweeping the Taurus down with the hill.

Demetri noticed in the rear-view mirror John's car being caught by the road collapse. Demetri smiled, looking at Laura, who sat bound in the back of the sedan. Laura's eyes widened with panic.

"The landslide caught your John," Demetri grinned as he pulled into Sergei's safehouse driveway on Robles Road off Empire Grade. She struggled, and Demetri nodded at Anatoly in the rearview mirror. Lev held Laura down while he pressed a cloth with chloroform to her mouth, knocking her out.

Sergei had a home nearby an Indian Yogi's residence. It was just down the mountain from Lockheed Martin. Its projects include the U.S. Navy's Trident II D5 Fleet Ballistic Missile (FBM) and the U.S. Missile Defense Agency's Terminal High Altitude Area Defense (THAAD) system. Sergei's surveillance team tracked shipments in and out of the facility.

"We will wait until the storm passes," Demetri announced.

**Felton-Empire Grade Slide**

Red lights flashed and reflected on the wet asphalt as fire and rescue vehicles crowded the road. A team of men pulled John from his car as he retrieved his dead cell phone.

"I need that charger and briefcase," he said as the medics tended to him, checking him for injuries.

**John and Laura's Rental**

The next morning, John paced the floor, wringing his hands in worry. His phone rang, and he dove toward it, answering it after the first ring.

"Is this John Nord?" Peter asked on the phone.

"Yes, it is." John said, "Who are you?"

"I am Peter Holland; I was working with George Camper on a story about cyber security." Peter replied, "George was attacked because of a computer disc you shared with him."

"They kidnapped my fiancé yesterday in Scotts Valley." John pleaded with Peter. "I am waiting to hear from them now. They are threatening to kill her."

"Take my number down." Peter recited his number. "And when you hear from them, do not agree to meet them anywhere they suggest. Think of a safe place with many people around."

"I have just the place for the exchange," John said. "They are calling me now."

"Call me back."

"Who are these people, John?" Laura's frightened voice came through the receiver.

John's eyes widened. "Laura? Laura, where are you?"

He was met with silence, followed by a deep, familiar Russian voice. "Now, let's play this smart," Sergei said. "We have her, and we want the disc."

John squeezed his eyes shut, pinching the bridge of his nose. "I… I have it."

"That is the first smart thing you've said," Sergei replied. "Now, you will drive to San Francisco, and we will meet in at the Marina."

## Rodriguez Conan 65 – San Francisco Yacht Club

Sergei leaned over the phone, and Laura glared at him angrily, her mouth gagged again.

"No, we are not. I have what YOU want!" John said. "We will meet in one hour in Oakland. Call me on my cell phone when you pass the toll booth on the Oakland Bay Bridge."

Sergei smirked. "Do not you start giving me orders, Mr. Nord. We have your Laura."

"Yeah, and I want to get her back as much as you need whatever is on this disc." John breathed heavily into the phone's receiver. "If you want it, you will get it on my turf!" He ended the call and called Peter.

Sergei shrugged as the call ended. "What does it matter? This way, I get the disc sooner. Dimitri?" he called for the Serbian. "We have a destination." Sergei smiled at Laura before entering the galley where Dimitre had just finished a pint can of dark ale.

" Dimitre?" Sergei said, in a quiet voice, "When we have the disc, kill them both."

## John and Laura's Rental

John reached Peter and told him the details of his meeting with Sergei.

"Mr. Holland, I will meet them in the Chapel of the Chimes at Mountain View Cemetery in one hour. An uncle of a friend of mine has a funeral today. He is being sent off by half of the Oakland Police force today."

"I will let Mike Murphy know about this and get some backup for you," Peter replied.

## Mountain View Cemetery

"Take 580 east and tell me when you're on it," John said into the phone. The phone was on the speaker, and he kept his eyes on the rearview mirror.

*"We are on 580,"* Sergei said.

"Get in the right lane and take Highway 24 east toward Berkeley. Take the Claremont exit," John instructed after a few moments.

"Okay, we are taking Claremont."

"Stay on Claremont until 51st Street. Turn right on 51st," John paused. "Tell me when you're passing Broadway."

*"We are passing Broadway."* Sergei's voice betrayed his growing annoyance.

"Slow down. You will be making a left turn on Piedmont."

"Da, we see it."

"Now find a place to park," John said, taking a deep breath to keep his nerves about him.

"A bit dramatic, young man," said the Russian. "We are parking."

## Chapel of the Chimes, Lobby

The Mountain View Cemetery had the spectacular Julia Morgan Buildings housing its mausoleum and the landmark Chapel of the Chimes in Piedmont. In 1928, they dedicated the building. The white exterior was a beautiful blend of Gothic and Romanesque details. John walked inside, spotting Jim Kelly in the lobby, and waved him over.

Jim's brow arched in surprise at the sight of him. John nodded, pointing to the farthest room beyond him. Jim gestured in understanding, following him down the hall.

"John," he said as he caught up to him. "What are you doing here? I thought you would be in Santa Cruz with Laura."

John turned to face Jim. "I need a big favor."

Jim took in his anxious face. "What is it?"

"Laura's in trouble," he said, keeping his voice low. "And I need your help."

Jim's eyes widened in question. "Anything, man!"

He nodded. "Laura was kidnapped yesterday at a meeting in Scotts Valley. This Russian has her and wants a data disc back. Sergei Marcov mixed up his disc with mine at the end of the video teleconference I ran for him on Monday. Please hold on to this until I get Laura back and then have you give it to the guy. Sergei is a tall Russian with a limp."

Jim gaped at him. "Why didn't you call the cops?"

"They're threatening to hurt her… or worse."

Jim nodded. "Okay. Okay, I'll do it."

John gave him a grateful smile. "You are a pal, I have them coming here, and I want them to meet me in the back garden. I will call your cell phone when to show up."

John turned on his heel and walked out of the room. Jim watched his friend retreat and called out to him. "Keep your eyes open and cover your ass!"

"Jim, you're the Head of my CYA!" John whispered back.

## Chapel of the Chimes

Off the reception, the foyer was a series of connected gardens. John stood by the reception desk, hidden by a depository of cremation vases that provided him with a view of the door. He held his phone to his ear.

Sergei and Boris escorted a terrified Laura between them. She looked frightened. Her eyes searched the lobby for signs of John.

"Good choice, young man. I see you like company," Sergei said into the phone. "Even though they are dead."

John nodded. "I am only interested in getting out of this alive with Laura," he instructed. "Go left in the lobby. Take the stairs through the four gardens."

"I am interested in your play of the cards," Sergei continued, following John's instructions, and turning left.

"You bring Laura, and my friend will hand you the disc when you let her go," John said.

**Foyer**

"How can I trust the disc is real?" Sergei asked.

"You know where I work and live," John retorted dryly.

Sergei was amused. "How can you trust me?"

"I don't!" John snapped. "Go down the stairs on your left."

**First Garden**

John had followed Sergei, taking an alternate route that would let him keep an eye on the Russian. Sergei and Laura walked down the stairs.

"Bring Laura to the last of the four gardens. Leave her sitting on the bench, and return to the first garden where my friend will give you the disc."

**Fourth Garden**

Laura sat down on the bench. Sergei still had the phone pressed to his ear. He looked around as John said into Sergei's ear, "Thank you! Return to the room where you came down the stairs, and Jim will meet you."

"You better deliver," Sergei threatened. "Or she's dead," as he exited the garden.

"I forgot to mention," John's tone was smug. "It is my friend's uncle's funeral today; he was a police officer killed on duty. Two hundred cops are coming in the doors right now. So do not get cute. Don't try to hold my friend or come back to this garden. Laura and I will be gone."

Jim approached Sergei as he mounted the stairs into the lobby. "Are you Sergei Marcov?" Jim asked.

"Yes, I am." Sergei replied, "You have something for me, young man?"

"Yes, I do; John gave me this for you." Jim handed the disc to Sergei. "Leave my friend and Laura alone. I have lots of friends around here for my uncle's funeral today.

"Jim!" Frank Holden walked up to Jim and Sergei. "I was Larry's partner when I was on the force. I wanted to give my condolences to you. Hello, Mr. Marcov, you and Boris need to come with me. I am Frank Holden, FBI." Frank pulled out his wallet and showed his identification.

"You cannot detain me; I have diplomatic immunity," Sergei replied, before he saw that Boris was already in custody. "But I will comply—the ambassador will straighten this out.

"We can sort this out in our offices," Frank replied.

# Six Months Later

**Mike Murphy**

Mike slipped an envelope under Peter Holland's door as quietly as possible. He did not want anyone at the Co-op to know he had been there.

**Spanish Inn, Carmel**

As Laura walked down the aisle in a fabulous wedding dress, John waited at the altar. Jim and Stephen were his best men.

"Thanks, Jim, for saving Laura and my ass."

"It was Larry coming through for us, even at his funeral. His partner, Frank Holden, joined the FBI and put the collar on Marcov and that Flattop beast. Too bad they had diplomatic immunity. They could only deport them."

**Peter and Happy's Bedroom**

"Peter, why don't you come to bed?" Happy said.

"I was wondering how bad this Y2K will be."

Happy propped herself up on an elbow. "It is not like you can do anymore. Your articles showed the danger to the third world and emerging markets." She shrugged. "George's code is going great guns on the Y2K backdoor on financial transactions, thanks to your exposé."

Peter nodded. "It looked like a one-hundred-billion-dollar sinkhole for the world's banks, best case."

"It is a shame we could not get the Justice Department to follow up on the investigation. Mike had it laid out so well."

Peter smiled wearily. "Well, if they opened that can of worms, they would have to worry about fundraising in the DNC and the National Labs. With Secretary O'Leary working for Kaiser, after the Rocky Flats security breakdowns. It would not have happened under Janet Reno."

"I'll call George," Happy said. "He invited us out on his boat today."

**Mike Murphy**

"Murphy here." He paused to listen before responding, "No, I will not be available for the oversight hearings, I retired five months ago, and my vacation starts today. My flight is in two hours." Mike ended the call by saying, "I have a score to settle in Mexico.

**George's Sailboat**

George's yacht was called the *Secure Lady*, a play on his transaction code. The Catalina 42 MKII is a sleek craft. George had ordered it with the self-reefing mainsail and jib. The cockpit had all the controls, so two could comfortably take the boat out. Happy called ahead to George on his cell phone, and he greeted them at the security gate of the Emeryville Marina.

"Happy," you're looking good as usual," George waved to his sister.

Happy smiled. "You are looking tired. Getting enough sleep?"

"In a word? No," George said. "A lot is going on, Happy. Peter, let's get everything squared away in the galley before we cast off."

Peter and Happy went below. This was Peter's third visit aboard George's 42-foot boat. He liked the cabin's layout. Peter iced down the beer and wine and rejoined George on the deck. The weather was beautiful.

"Peter," George called out. "Do you mind freeing the lines?"

"Glad to," he said. "A great idea getting out today."

George nodded. "I need it as much as anyone."

As they cleared the Marina, George steered port between the channel markers. They regularly dredged the channel because the mudflats and tides continued filling it in. The wind was slack until mid-afternoon.

The Great Central Valley became an atmospheric vacuum when the summer heat pulled the marine air through the Golden Gate. Using the motor, George cruised toward Angel Island, eight miles away. It took a little over an hour to reach the calm wind shadow of the large island. The Bay Bridge's causeway section and cantilever section were to the south. George took a course that ran close to Treasure Island. He always enjoyed seeing the historic World's Fair buildings. The city of San Francisco hosted a World's Fair on the artificial island known as Treasure Island.

The landfill for the island came from building the double-decker tunnel through Yerba Buena Island. The Fair celebrated the Golden Gate and the Bay Bridges' completion.

George dropped anchor on the leeward side of Angle Island, and Happy brought lunch on deck. "George, you look exhausted; what is driving you all hours?" she asked.

"We have this upcoming rollout with twenty key markets, and our core code is running the network operation centers and the vertical market giveaways. Peter, can I have one of your beers?" Peter gave Happy one of those know-it-alls looks.

She gave him one of those 'don't push your luck' eyebrows. "It is so big, and with such market penetration, I am stunned. After your article on the Russian Mafia's Y2K plans, my application is going great guns. Just who was your source, Peter?"

"I can't tell you." Peter said, avoiding meeting his eyes.

"I understand you have to protect your sources." said George, prompting a little more.

"George — I do not know; I had an anonymous envelope left at my flat. I never knew who was behind the information."

"The next thing I know is, I am doing a deal for twenty million units." George said with a smile.

"Twenty million units?" Happy asked.

"Yes, your friends have selected ten markets for e-commerce. They are giving out outrageous machines, high-powered desktops, massive drive space, and fast communications just for signing up with a nonproprietary hosting service. It boggles the mind."

"That is their entire production run; every machine they make, your code is on it."

"Bill Gates would love to have a one hundred percent market share of this many units."

"Yeah, I know, with CompuServe offering four-hundred-dollar rebates, and now EarthLink offering iMacs, just for signing, for three years of internet service."

"Well, I do not understand their business model. It just does not pencil it out. It makes the Japanese market share-buying look like Robber Baron Kindergarteners."

"Peter and I had the same thoughts."

"It is on the scale of Microsoft giving away Exchange to own the market. Have you bothered to look at Netscape's desktop share lately?"

"But why the hyper-aggressive stance? They cannot make money; we are talking billions of dollars to feed the machine. That is one big market share buy-in."

"There isn't any part of the plan that makes sense other than to get their machines into key industries."

"It would be a fantastic way to build a back door into the world of commerce, except my code is in the way! The wind is picking up, Avast Ye, mates, it is time to unfurl the jib."

"Aye, aye, Captain."

The sailing was terrific; the wind picked up to twenty-five knots. They made several high-speed runs between Alcatraz and Vista Point in Marin; the tides were slack, and the Delta Breeze was the strongest. Windsurfers used the wake of the Catalina to jump their boards and practice closing skills and footwork. Kayaks shared water. After a half dozen good runs, it was time to head into the Marina.

"Coming about!"

"Aye, aye!"

"Furling the mainsail!" Managing the sails from the cockpit is a real luxury on a sailboat. Using the diesel to keep the bow in the wind, they cranked in the canvas sails and turned into port.

As they tied up the boat, Peter noticed the fog pouring over the Golden Gate Bridge and enveloping Sutro Tower.

"Thanks for the great day, George."

"You're welcome, Peter. I am glad you and Happy are a good fit for each other."

"I couldn't say it any better."

"Happy, you better take care of Peter. I have him trained now; I do not want to break in another swabbie."

"George, it was a wonderful time. Thanks for the day. Call me if you are going to visit Aunt Em." Before going home, they stopped for supplies at Trader Joe's and the new Office Depot at the new box retail center off Christie Avenue.

Peter struggled with the packages as Happy said, "Peter, wait up; I'll get to the front door." Peter almost lost the grip of the packages, stepping through the entry door. Happy dashed by and got to the other door.

*'Front door… front door.'* Peter thought to himself. He made his way through the multi-level flat to the kitchen table, with the womanly touches Happy made. "Thanks for getting the door, sweetie."

"Before we make dinner, I want a shower and then a little love commerce with you," she teased.

Peter stopped in his tracks. "That's it! What's George's number? Can you dial it for me?"

She did as he asked, holding out the phone. "Peter, what is going on? Here, it is ringing."

"George? Peter. You mentioned the back door. What about a front door?"

**UUNet Network Operation Center**

The UUNet's Technical Operation Manager just finished the installation of the twenty OC 194 network servers. The Cisco routers were online. On the large display wall, CCC switchers allowed the six network managers direct control of all the servers. The RGBHY switchers are routing the five hundred new Internet servers' display cards to the sixteen screens. The servers were screamers; it did not hurt them, each having eight Merced processors.

Ted Truant realized UUNet, a division of MCI/Worldcom, was happy the budget was coming in way under projections. It was one of the fastest-track projects the company put up. They lit the pipe three months after they signed the lease with the Staubach Company. The high-brightness Panasonic LCD projectors were helping the budget as well. He was about to turn the center over to operations. They scored two significant retailers using LivePerson technology, and the brass was anxious to start the revenue stream.

**Peter's Loft**

"Yes, front door; you mentioned a back door was impossible with your code. If you were the administrator? The code, all the machines in the loop had your code, your passkey?"

"Only…"

END

# Ten Years Later

### General Chen

General Chen's work led to several developments. He was elevated to one of the twenty-four members of The Politburo of the Chinese Communist Party.

### Oak Ridge National Labs

Jiang Mianheng, son of former Chinese president Jiang Zemin, visited Oak Ridge in 2010 and brokered a cooperation agreement with the lab. The deal gave the Chinese Academy of Sciences, which has a staff of 50,000, the plans for the Molten Salt Reactor and a Thorium reactor. In January 2011, Jiang signed a protocol with the Department of Energy outlining the terms of joint energy research with the academy. China intends to own the Global IP Rights to low-cost nuclear energy.

### Rare Earth Elements

China cuts off Japan's supply of rare earth elements, enforcing its signal to technology companies that they must move to China if they want secure access to components. Xi Jinping's family holds $400 million in rare earth value chain assets.